STARSTRUCK ROMANCE
and OTHER HOLLYWOOD TAILS

ALSO BY JULIA DUMONT:

Sleeping With Dogs and Other Lovers, A Second Acts Novel - Book 1

"The misunderstandings and mischief will keep readers turning pages... erotic adventure for readers more interested in an entertaining read than deep thought."

– *Kirkus Reviews*

"Think Stephanie Plum meets *Sex and the City* wearing *Fifty Shades of Grey* – L.A. style. In Julia Dumont's funny and erotic romantic novel, *Sleeping with Dogs and Other Lovers*, sparks fly as matchmaker extraordinaire Cynthia Amas tries to make sense of her own increasingly complicated -- and steamy -- love life."

– *Kindle Nation*

"If *50 Shades of Grey* was a bit too kinky for you but you'd like a hot sexy story, this is it! ...Cynthia and her "bad-boy lover" Max's intense sexual connection was a highlight, but I also loved the wacky fun that ensued with her friends and crazy mom."

– *Amazon*

www.TruLoveStories.com
Where Passionistas Play!

BroadLit

July 2012

Published by

BroadLit ®
14011 Ventura Blvd.
Suite 206 E
Sherman Oaks, CA 91423

ISBN 978-0-9855404-5-6

Produced in the United States of America.

Visit us online at www.TruLOVEstories.com

To all the women, like me, who are taking a
second chance at love, life and new ventures.

I would like to thank first and always, Barbara Weller, Cynthia Cleveland and Nancy Cushing-Jones, who are not only the inspiration for this story, but also my dedicated and crazy but brilliant editors and the best girlfriends ever. I also want to thank my husband, Dilbert, whose nightly visits to the neighborhood donut shop sustained me throughout those long nights burning the midnight oil at my computer.

*S*TARSTRUCK ROMANCE
and OTHER HOLLYWOOD TAILS

A **SECOND ACTS** NOVEL

by JULIA DUMONT

A BROADLIT BOOK

Day 1, Chapter 1

Rain was pounding so hard on the convertible top, Cynthia Amas could no longer hear herself think, let alone make out the lyrics of the frantic rock song blasting from the radio. The wipers were on high, but it was futile. They seemed like frantic little tyrannosaurus rex arms, ill equipped for keeping the deluge at bay. In all her years of living in Los Angeles, Cynthia had never seen this kind of downpour. Visibility: zero. Traffic on Sepulveda Boulevard, normally an effective shortcut, had come to a complete halt. She was going to be late for the most important meeting of Second Acts Dating Service's four-month history. She had no idea that this was the first of two very eventful days that would shake her world.

Cynthia had swung by her mother's house to drop off some headshots of potential dates. She had made it a personal and professional mission to find a match for her mother. She loved her dearly, but one, she wanted her to find happiness, and two, and more importantly, she desperately needed someone else to take over at least some of the duties associated with her mother's sky-high maintenance. No, sky-high was a gross understatement. More like beyond the Milky Way, in a whole other galaxy. Obviously, matchmaking her mom was a time-and-energy-sucking proposition. She would have preferred to do it via email, but, for her mother, that was a non-starter. Cynthia had given her countless tutorials on the computer and had even spent an entire afternoon coaching her on how to navigate the Second Acts website, but Marjorie Amas was adamantly opposed to retaining any knowledge that might potentially save Cynthia time and aggravation. Aggravating her daughter was one of her strong suits. Of course, it also had something to do with the fact that Margie wanted to *see* her. Cynthia understood that, and she did enjoy her mother's company at least some of the time, but making a trip over to the valley in the middle of morning rush hour was unbelievably inconvenient . . . and the timing couldn't have been worse. It's not every day one has a private consultation with the number-one movie box office draw for the last three years running.

Jack Stone had two Oscars, one for acting and one for

directing. He had one Tony and one Emmy. He'd had one failed marriage to his high school sweetheart—long before the gods of celebrity had plucked him from small-town Colorado obscurity twenty years ago. Since then he'd pretty much slept with every starlet he'd laid eyes on. There was endless speculation about the women he dated and whether any of them would ever settle him down, but so far there was zero evidence that they could. He was one of those handsome men who seem to get sexier and sexier with every passing year. It was maddening to women. While they had to spend increasingly more time getting ready to leave the house in the morning, Stone was the kind of guy who could not shave, not get enough sleep, not dress up, and still win World's Sexiest Man . . . which he had done four times. So far. In a recent incident, his neighbor, a twenty-seven year-old Eastern European supermodel, had caught a glimpse of him walking Scarlet O'Hara, his wheaten terrier, and promptly crashed her Porsche into a palm tree. She was severely injured, but not from the accident. Her *feelings* were hurt when he didn't ask her into his house.

"Stupid model," Cynthia's mother had said at the time, "if it had been me, I would have feigned a faint and hitched a ride in his arms to his couch while I waited for the tow truck to arrive."

"Believe me," Cynthia had replied, "I know you would." Since Cynthia's father had died, her mother's history with men was checkered with shenanigans like that. She had been kicked out of two doctors' practices for basically molesting said doctors.

Meanwhile, Second Acts had really taken off. The website was bustling with traffic. Membership had quadrupled in the past few months. Despite the sorry state of the economy, or maybe *because* of it, men and women were more desperate than ever to hook up. Not necessarily hoping to get married, but definitely looking for something that lasts. She had been remarkably successful at matching people. She had hardly any complaints and only failed miserably with one client: her good friend, Lolita Albion. Cynthia didn't take it as a true failure, because in this case, the customer was always *wrong*.

But as difficult as Lolita was as a prospective match, she had been very helpful as a friend and at drumming up business. She talked up Second Acts constantly at Dog Groomer to the Stars, her high-end Beverly Hills shop, handing out cards, and even directing her own dogs to spread the word in the canine world. King, Max, and Wilfredo——Great Dane, Irish Wolfhound, and Chihuahua, respectively——were social animals. The dog chatter in there was akin to a nail salon——nonstop hot and heavy gossip . . . the perfect place for promoting anything, really. And everything King, Max, and Wilfredo learned, they passed on to Lolita, who passed it on to Cynthia. It was a sweet arrangement.

It was the most exclusive salon, spa, and all around puppy paradise in L.A., which was saying a lot. Located on the most prestigious commercial block of Beverly Hills, it successfully catered to the nearly insatiable obsession of the rich and/or famous to over-pamper their pooches. It almost seemed like her clients heaped more luxury upon their furry "children" than they did their actual ones. Lolita wasn't sure she approved of this, but she certainly did wholeheartedly where it counted, on her bottom line. She also owned an incredible boarding facility called Bed Breakfast and Bone (a double entendre lost on some of the stodgier clients, but right in the zone for the younger ones who after all are the future). It was situated on a perfect two-acre parcel, up the hill from the salon, just beyond the Beverly Hills Hotel and nearly on par with it in terms of opulence and amenities. The four-legged clients could literally sit poolside with a view of the human hotel guests lounging below by *their* pool. The dogs enjoyed an indoor-outdoor experience that resembled world-class resort. The small staff catered to every doggy whim. When prospective clients toured the grounds they often remarked that maybe they should check in *with* their dogs instead of flying halfway around the world for a potentially inferior vacation experience.

Max, King, and Wilfredo spent time in both locations, and were always hyper-aware of the comings and goings and needs of the other dogs *and* their humans. They had been a big help to Lolita all her life and recently in business. She was more than happy to have them help out Cynthia as well.

But they were occasionally problematic. King was prone to vanishing and then reappearing in all kinds of unlikely locations——somehow unhindered by locked doors and high walls, scaring the bejeezus out of innocent bystanders——especially those who happened to take a liking to Lolita. Cynthia's friend Diego was nearly chased out of town when King discovered Lolita and him in a romantic entanglement. Diego had been in an extremely vulnerable position. As in *naked*. Exposed body parts. Exposed *tender* body parts. Diego escaped intact, but suffered horrible nightmares for weeks.

Max seemed to have a peculiar knack for just plain knowing things he shouldn't know. It wasn't just that he understood human language——multiple human languages——he also seemed to comprehend things that went unsaid, like some kind of doggy mind reader.

Wilfredo was more of an all-around troublemaker . . . a thief, a pick pocket, you name it. If he were human, he'd have been in jail by now. He was big on rooting through garbage and files and dragging in all kinds of both important and completely *unimportant* ephemera to Lolita. He once delivered a diary he'd pilfered from the purse of a starlet who happened to be walking her Afghan hound past the shop. It also contained her passport, drug tests, and love letters to three separate, very-married United States Senators. Lolita returned everything to her, but not before finding out she was trying desperately to turn over a new leaf and get serious about trying to find a good man- vital information Lolita immediately passed on to Cynthia. Lolita had also found another client for herself . . . and Wilfredo, an Afghan girlfriend.

"Sweeties, listen up," Lolita would say. "Just give me the who, what, where, why, when. Don't break or enter or rob or murder anyone on my account, okay? What do you say? Is that clear?" They would all nod and promise, but despite their good intentions and extraordinary abilities, they were still dogs, after all . . . ruled by instinct and id.

If a squirrel came along, all bets were off. Or a man with romantic designs on Lolita.

But overall, the grooming shop and doggy hotel provided one effective pooch pipeline to exclusive eligibles. Which, in a roundabout way, was how Jack Stone got involved. Cynthia was still incredulous that this major movie star wanted or needed help in finding someone. She guessed that 99% of the female population of the U.S. would be happy to date him. But he'd said he was tired of women falling in love with him because of their preconceived media-made notion of who he was and what he wanted in life. He'd said that he was not "Jack Stone" . . . nobody could be. He wanted Cynthia to handle it and his famous face would have to be kept out of the equation, at least until after the dates had been agreed upon. He wanted the prospective suitors to choose him based on qualities other than those that could be gleaned from the silver screen or tabloid television.

The phone rang and Cynthia inserted her ear buds.

"Hello, Lolita. No, I'm not there yet." She knew that her friend was on pins and needles, waiting for a full report on Jack Stone. "No, I don't know what his house is like yet. I don't know what he's wearing yet. Plus, I'm stuck on Sepulveda in the kind of rain that makes you want to build a large boat and start collecting animals. I have to get off the phone to let them know that I'll be a little late."

"Cynthia! You need to leave early for this kind of thing!"

"I left *incredibly* early! The weatherman didn't exactly predict a meteorological event of biblical proportions."

"But Cynthia, for this kind of meeting you leave a day

ahead and *camp out*. And you need to find out about you know what."

Cynthia *did* know what. She knew the rumors anyway . . . about the extraordinary size of Jack Stone's *endowment*. All these reports are rooted in hearsay of course, but according to some, his wanker out-wanked everyone. In recent years, the big-schlong contenders were Colin Farrell, Liam Neeson, Ewan MacGregor, and a few others. Further back in Hollywood history, Sinatra was always mentioned (supposedly according to '50s starlet Ava Garner, "of his 112 pounds, 12 was Frank and 100 was cock"). But it was the comedian Milton Berle who was always considered the man to beat. The famous story about him was that he got challenged in a bar, made a very large bet, and then, when confronted with the other man's oversized salami, "only took out enough to win."

But lately, at least for the last few years, in countless tantalizing, but ultimately inconclusive tabloid beach shots, all eyes were below Jack Stone's belt, trying to get a glimpse, a hint, some indication of the dimensions of his dong, the weight of his willy, the heft of his hammer.

"You have to ask him," said Lolita. "I mean, jeez, it's what everyone wants to know."

"And by 'everyone' do you mean everyone named *Lolita Adriana Albion?*" asked Cynthia.

"No, I mean 50% of the Earth's population. But come to think of it, it's probably closer to 99%. Whatever…at least ask him. Remember, this only happened because of me."

She was right. It actually started with Wilfred Ames, a short, stocky character actor who had been bringing his five schnauzers into Lolita's shop for a year or so. Wilfred was chatting with Lolita one day, obviously trying to pick her up. He wasn't too subtle: "As my character Chuckles Roselli said to Karen Biali, a one-time *Hustler* centerfold, in the low-budget mob comedy *The Godfather of the Bride*, 'Honey, if you spend a little equity shaking your moneymaker for me, you'll get a good return on your investment." Sure, he was crude, but he was feeling pretty desperate. His wife had left him. Well, not exactly *left* him. He had been on a shoot in Canada and came home as a surprise one weekend, except the surprise was on him instead. He found his wife in bed with his sister. His *older* sister…the one with the moustache. Surprise!

Anyway, Lolita wasn't about to go out with Wilfred. "I have a strict policy against dating men with five o'clock shadows immediately after shaving," she'd said. "He looks like he had a five o'clock shadow in the womb." But she was nice to him and convinced him to sign up for Second Acts. It worked out spectacularly well. Cynthia hooked Wilfred up with Denise Kopaki, a casting director. Suddenly his love life *and* career shot through the roof. On his next movie, he mentioned it to another actor, who mentioned it to another, and another, and eventually someone mentioned it to Jack Stone. Jack's pretty young assistant brought his dog in, who talked to Lolita's dogs (who have powers far beyond those of their canine colleagues), and the rest is history.

"Okay, okay, Lolita. I know they did some doggy dishing about their famous master's love life, but look, I've gotta go." Her good friend occasionally drove her completely bonkers. More than occasionally actually.

Let's see . . . recent calls . . . here we go.

Beep. Ringing . . .

"Hello, it's Mariana." This was Jack Stone's personal assistant. Or one of them. He may have had an army of them for all she knew.

"Hi, Mariana, it's Cynthia. I'm going to be a little late. Stuck in a lake on Sepulveda."

"Oh, no problem. He's not back from his run yet anyway."

Cynthia looked out into the torrent. "He's running in this monsoon?"

"Rain, shine, snow, and hail. Hasn't missed a run in eleven years. When he sprained his ankle on *The Big Nowhere* he ran with crutches for two weeks."

"Wow," said Cynthia, "that's dedication."

"That's insane as far as I'm concerned," laughed Mariana, "but that's Jack. He thinks he's Superman."

Cynthia laughed too. She found it refreshing that his assistant would joke openly about her boss and she got the feeling that he wouldn't care at all that their relationship was friendly and playful that way. She instantly felt less intimidated about meeting him. She had known lots of movie folk during her time as a marketing exec at two major Hollywood studios and there were plenty of bosses who no one would even think of making a joke about. There's little lighthearted comradery in an office run on high-octane fear.

As traffic came to a complete halt near the Getty Center, she thought about how she had been taking these excursions in exclusive neighborhoods much more often lately. Second Acts had been growing in leaps and bounds, but success with Jack Stone could bring the enterprise to a whole new level. She fantasized about Stone dropping her name or mentioning the business on the red carpet or in the Polo Lounge within earshot of just the right group of A-list singles . . . the kind of promotion you cannot buy.

Suddenly, she heard a rattle and whir and looked over just in time to see a handsome young man, probably in his mid-twenties, whiz by on a bike, making every driver in every car feel like a mindless robot for his slavish devotion to the traffic-shackled automobile. Cynthia barely caught the cyclist's profile, his dark curls in the breeze, and the silhouette of his angular physique, but it was enough to trigger a visceral and deeply sensual recollection. Cynthia was prone to stuck-in-traffic sexual fantasy anyway, but this kid was the spitting image of Pete Blatt.

She instantly felt her face flush. Fever spread through every erogenous zone. This was crazy. Cynthia had gone to high school with Pete and they'd fooled around only once. She had come to think of it as the Pisco Pete Incident. It involved the aforementioned potent Peruvian libation, a large bag of Cheetos, and a fun, drunken swirl of messy sexual exploration. It was a deeply flawed experience, but that was irrelevant now. It was also an intensely potent sense memory that immediately seized her imagination and lit her libido like erotic wildfire.

She imagined herself speeding along on a bike too, following Pete or this Pete-like stranger, down around the bend, flying past the stalled serpent of bored commuters on their way to boring offices...all desperate to get there, but destined to be even more desperate to leave the minute they arrived. Coasting downhill, the wind cooling their flushed faces, they slalomed their way through Westwood and tumbled off their bikes onto soft grass under a sprawling oak somewhere. Their hearts, already pounding from the ride, now pumped with a whole different sort of syncopation as they covered each other with wet kisses and caresses. Their skin tasted of salt and soon they whispered and sighed through trembling lips that their swelling urge to merge was probably best not consummated there in the middle of the U.C.L.A. quad. But this was no obstacle to their overwhelming lust. Running, giggling, and gasping up the stairwell of the first available dorm, they searched for a spot, a secluded alcove, an abandoned couch or bunk or bit of carpet, where they could claw each others' clothes to shreds, as if their lives depended on it. They were frantic to see, feel, taste, screw, shudder, and scream like it really mattered. Like it was the only thing that mattered. His hands were hot and his lips starving as he lavished her breasts with the kind of profoundly engaged kisses that penetrate deep below the surface. Her alert, swollen, pertness, like tender pink sensors, sent tingling pulses of pleasure through her every molten molecule. His adoring eyes and mouth traveled in slow motion to her belly, then hip, then down, up, and over her supple mound of madly aching love, her mons pubis...deep into the sweet honey-soaked delirium of her thighs, temperature rising, warm mouth breathing gently, whispering sweetly, famished tongue devouring thoroughly, pushing and pleasing to convulsive climax almost instantly.

Her back arching, she cried out and shed a delicious tear as she took his head in her hands, clinging to his curls, pulling and pleading with him to bring the game back up, to come back, to *please* come back to her and come *in* her. Please. Now. Please. But he insisted on teasing her even more, thoroughly tasting and tantalizing until the tremors became unbearable and she moaned and screamed for him to *please, god, stop*. And then, finally, rising from the depths like a primordial love revolving to the next stage of sexual transformation, he clamored toward his inevitable, instinctual prize. But then he paused again at her breasts, determined to torment her and himself through maddening, nearly sadistic *and* masochistic restraint...insisting on delaying what they both desperately desired. Finally he was near enough and she reached out and just barely stroked his throbbing erection with her fingertips, causing twitches of spasmodic anticipation...coaxing, then demanding he bring it and bring it *now*, goddamn it. Which he did at long last with uncompromising, otherworldly force, surging and thrusting, giving and taking everything, everything, everything. Again and again and again. This time, her legs wrapped tightly around him, she screamed louder and longer than before, writhing in ecstasy beneath him, collapsing with him, he within her, dying what she was quite sure was the most exquisite simultaneous petite mort in all of petite mort history. Actually, nothing petite about it.

And that's when Cynthia realized that half of Los Angeles was honking behind her, a cacophony of frustration that she'd caused them to miss the traffic light, now nearly as red as her face. She was seriously flustered from her excursion into ecstasy.

Hell, they're just jealous. I mean, who wouldn't want to experience that kind of fully realized sexual fantasy in the time it takes for a light to change?

She finally turned onto Sunset, the traffic breaking up, and wound her way east, to the west gate of Bel Air at Bellagio Road. She'd been to Bel Air many times before and had almost always gotten lost. A couple of years ago, she was on the way to a meeting with a starlet and came to a dead end at the massive gate of the Aaron Spelling mansion. She recognized it from the photos that had been plastered all over the news when it had been up for sale a few years earlier. She'd gotten out of her car and peered through the fence, but couldn't see much of the $150 million abode's 57,000 square feet. She had calculated that she could fit her apartment inside it thirty-eight times.

Thirty seconds up the hill from heavy Sunset traffic she found and then lost herself in a maze of wooded, winding roads lined with stone walls and high gates guarding old-world mansions, modern architectural masterpieces, and a few gaudy monstrosities too. Immense wealth is not necessarily an indicator of taste. Rain was still coming down in buckets and each twist and turn through these well-appointed foothills of the Santa Monica Mountains brought a new torrent of ocean-bound rainwater. Cynthia imagined she was driving against the current of an ultra-exclusive river. Address after elite address: Roscomare Road, Chalton Road, Chantilly, Somera.

Finally, as she rounded the turn onto Portofino Place, the rain let up and a blast of sunshine broke through the clouds, causing a small patch of red clay tile roof to glow through the glistening foliage, as if illuminated from within. In a city full of astonishingly diverse microclimates, it was like Jack Stone lived in a magical kingdom all his own, unaffected by the whims of the weather gods that torment mere mortals——even apparently rich ones residing in his neighborhood.

Cynthia slid out of the car and was reaching for the button on the stone-gray intercom, tastefully overgrown with ivy, when she heard the crunch of running shoes on gravel.

"Cynthia, I presume?" asked Jack Stone, out of breath, pushing his drenched hair from his forehead, looking exactly like he did in the movies, except soaking wet. Some people caught in the rain resemble wet rats, but not him.

Cynthia said nothing for a moment. She stared at the soaked and comfortably worn-out t-shirt clinging to his biceps, chest, and abdomen. Feeling a tad nonplussed, as if she'd wandered into a private, informal wet t-shirt contest, she averted her eyes downward, only to focus briefly at the equally drenched jersey running shorts that delineated his powerful thighs. *His legs. God I love strong legs with just the right amount of hair. Manly, not gorilla-y. I can't believe I'm evaluating the leg hair of Jack Stone. Pinch me. No, don't pinch me . . . that will send me over the edge.* She, of course, thought of Lolita's question and quickly scanned for answers that she did not get. But she found herself flashing to one of those short sexual fantasies that begins and ends before you know it. *Wow, I got there fast. Did I just visibly shudder? Did he notice? Hold on, snap out of it. This is more than a little inappropriate since I'm here to discuss how to match him with somebody else, not myself.*

"Right," she finally said with a smile, "I'm Cynthia. And you are? . . ." *Oh, God, I did not really pretend to not recognize him. I meant to be playful in the same way his assistant had been, but if I've learned anything about movie stars, they're all pretty sensitive and they really do hate if they're not recognized, despite their protests to the contrary.*

"Me?" he asked incredulously.

Oh, god . . . he is that sensitive.

"Name's Justin Bieber," he announced with a deadly serious expression.

Cynthia blurted out a huge guffaw. It was one of those absurdly masculine laughs that occasionally escapes from the mouth of an attractive woman suddenly channeling a cigar-chomping mayor of a Midwestern city. Not exactly what you're hoping for while attempting to flirt with an international film sensation.

But Stone laughed just as loudly and put his hand on her shoulder like they were old friends and Cynthia instantly felt comfortable. If any meeting could simultaneously dispose of a movie star's hermetically sealed image and replace it with something even better—much better—this was it.

"Well, Beebs," she said, "pleased to meet you." She was happy to have something to call him.

"C'mon," he said, punching in the combination on the gate, causing it to open slowly and silently, "let's get something hot to drink."

She parked her car over to the side, got out, and they descended the long driveway, the expanse of property unfolding before them. Cynthia was always amazed that these kinds of massive park-like parcels existed all over Los Angeles. Lush forest, deep moss, ferns, flowers, stone walls, babbling brook . . . you name it. Except for the occasional palm and a sweet blend of jasmine and orange blossom in her nostrils, this was pure English countryside. She was fully aware of the vast urban sprawl somewhere beyond all this, the real world hidden by an exotic façade.

Cynthia heard a loud thwack and turned to see a curly-coated mocha-brown terrier bounding toward them. She'd emerged from a large doggy door set in the lower half of the massive, ornately carved front door of the residence. Scarlett O'Hara, coming at you. This was one happy dog. She galloped and bounded, apparently half thoroughbred and half kangaroo, and vaulted——extended like a genuine super dog, for the last ten or twelve feet——into Stone's arms, who received her like a gigantic furry football.

"Scarlett, Scarlett, Scarlett," he said, laughing again—laughter obviously came easily to him—as the dog slobbered every square inch of his face and neck. "Hold it, hold it, hold it . . . not the eyeball, not the eyeball . . . Scarlett, not the eyeball!" He hugged her like a woman . . . turning and waltzing circuitously toward the house, and then turned her loose to lead the way.

The house. Cynthia guessed eight or ten thousand square feet of old-world elegance. It was the kind of Spanish revival built in the 1920's that looked authentically, romantically, heartbreakingly old-old, like from-the-eighteenth-century old. The ivy, the distressed shutters, the aged and mottled surfaces—if you didn't know better, you'd think it was abandoned and in a state of arrested decay, having naturally reached this state of glorious, glamorous deterioration on its own, with help from only Father Time and Mother Nature. But Cynthia knew that its imperfections had been intentionally, meticulously rendered this way, that the high-priced decorator——no doubt on permanent retainer, stopping by for regular trompe l'oeil touch-ups——had an eye for delicious decrepitude. They entered the foyer, which was somehow gloriously understated, despite the magnificent staircase and vaulted ceiling. The colors were muted, again as if time had taken a beautiful toll upon them . . . but of course it was recently painted this way. The entire assignment had been handled more like a Hollywood set than a personal residence. But it was unbelievably beautiful.

They entered the kitchen, which rambled downward with the contour of the hill, into a large common area, opening to a patio and sprawling yard. Scarlett O'Hara was already lounging poolside. The far wall was all multi-paned windows——creating a breathtaking grid of the Los Angeles panorama below——from West Hollywood on the left, to Westwood Village below, to the south beaches, Catalina

Island, and the gleaming Pacific. She could see other islands that she couldn't identify . . . the Channel Islands, maybe? It felt like she could see Hawaii, even though she wasn't so bad at geography to believe that could be true. It was just that the view was so impossibly intoxicating, it was easy to believe impossible things. Maybe God had a better view than this . . . maybe not.

"So," Jack said, taking two white coffee mugs from a cupboard, "is coffee good? I have other options if you want. Tea? Anything but cappuccino. I've never used that damn machine. I'd ask Mariana, but she's on break."

"That damn machine" was a restaurant-style cappuccino machine that looked more expensive than most houses. Cynthia actually knew how to use one. She had worked in coffee shops during college and considered offering, but then thought seeming like a know-it-all at this stage would probably be a mistake.

"Coffee is perfect," she said, sliding onto a stool at the long black-stone-topped counter. Was it onyx? Do they even make counters out of onyx? It's not that pricey as a stone in a necklace, but what could an onyx countertop cost? Whatever it was, it was no doubt negligible in this neighborhood.

"You know what," he said, looking at his goose bump-covered arm and shivering slightly. "I think I'd better slip into something more . . . umm . . . *dry*. So help yourself. There's milk in the fridge, plus maybe a few other semi-edibles. I am a single man, after all, so you never know what you'll encounter in there." He disappeared around a corner.

There was a distant splash and Cynthia looked out to see a beautiful woman standing poolside. Her bikini almost matched her skin color. Cynthia had to squint to confirm that she was indeed wearing anything at all. The girl dove in, causing the tiniest splash. *Mariana maybe?*

She opened the Sub-Zero and Stone was right. It had single dude written all over it. But single dude with taste: three Bass Ales, seven Pink Lady apples, a gigantic tub of homemade peanut butter, one large bowl containing countless varieties of Mediterranean olives, several bottles of extremely expensive champagne, a very large block of sharp Vermont cheddar cheese——a knife plunged deep, dramatically, into its top like Excalibur, and the biggest can of gourmet chocolate syrup she'd ever seen. In the freezer: three brands of vodka and nine flavors of Ben and Jerry's ice cream, one of which was named after him.

She added milk to her coffee, stirring with her finger, and gazed at the girl in the pool . . . swimming a languid backstroke.

"Yeah," said Stone, returning to the kitchen, now dressed

in jeans and a white t-shirt. Devastating in a sophisticated cowboy sort of way. "Mariana likes to swim."

"She seems great," said Cynthia, adding milk and stirring. "I mean she's funny on the phone."

"Yeah, she is great," he replied. "But I fired her. Yesterday."

"Really, why? Too much swimming on the job?" Cynthia realized this was none of her business, but she was genuinely curious. He may have fired her, but as of this morning she was still working for him. Mariana seemed like a fantastic employee and if *she* hadn't worked out, Cynthia wondered just how judgmental Stone would be toward her and her matchmaking efforts. "Never mind, I don't know why I even asked that."

"Oh, it's no problem," he said, taking a slow, deliberate sip from his cup. "She's great at her job. And the swimming is a perk I'm totally fine with. It wasn't a good fit for other reasons."

"Oh, okay," she said. It was obvious that these reasons were more personal in nature and she wasn't about to pry.

"But I should probably tell you," he continued, "because it's relevant to what we're meeting about."

Okay, here we go.

"This is weird," he continued, "I'm not boasting or anything. I'm really not like that. There is no way in hell I'd be telling you this except that you're here to help with my love life. This whole celebrity thing is a curse. I'm not being coy. I adore being adored. It's why I got into this racket. I don't whine about paparazzi or autographs or any of that. It comes with the territory and, look around, the territory is pretty nice. But the thing is, women fall in love with me. Almost all of them."

"C'mon, really?" asked Cynthia, "Almost *all* of them?" She actually totally believed this. She was feeling something for him already. But she was not about to say so.

"I know, it's crazy," he said. "I try to avoid it, but it's literally unavoidable. If I try to discourage them, even if I get kind of mean to them, it only makes it worse. Mariana has been working for me for a month. Like you said, she's great. Intelligent, talented . . . she went to Brown for god's sake. She has an amazing boyfriend. Well . . . *had*. She dropped him a week ago. Yesterday I went out to a meeting and came back early. I found her lying on her back on top of my covers, dressed only in my briefs . . . fast asleep. An empty bottle of Dom Perignon lay next to her like a tiny sleeping companion. She was holding an autographed photo of me to her bare breasts. Two of the most perfect breasts I have ever seen, by the way. I mean, works of art. Breathtaking. They literally took my breath away for a moment there. I covered her up and let her sleep. I had done nothing to encourage this behavior. I truly believe she was completely sane when I hired her. This is the terrible power of celebrity. Cynthia, you need to help me find someone who is immune to that. Someone who hasn't seen my movies, who hasn't been brainwashed into thinking I'm some kind of perfect man or something, because, let me tell you, I'm not."

"Wow," said Cynthia, wondering what he thought his imperfections were, because, frankly, she wasn't seeing any. She also had doubts that she could find someone like that, someone impervious to his public persona. I mean, where would she find her, on Mars? Jack Stone couldn't walk down the street anywhere in the world without being mobbed and adored by women *and* men. Maybe Antarctica, but she could totally see penguins having the hots for him. "Well," she continued, "maybe you should list these imperfections, just to get them out in the open. That way, prospective women would have to accept you warts and all, you know? So, what do you say? Show me some warts. Why do I have a feeling even your warts are handsome?"

Jack Stone smiled. "No, no, far from it," he said, gazing deeply into Cynthia's eyes. No one had spoken to him quite like this and he liked it. "I have plenty of very ugly warts. How much time do you have?" he asked, lifting his coffee cup and clinking it with hers.

"All day," she replied, unclasping her watch and putting it in her pocket.

Mariana walked in from the patio. She was drying her long brown hair with a black towel, leaving a trail of drips across the floor. Her body was ridiculously perfect. Her tiny wet bikini barely qualified as clothing. The cream-colored fabric was beyond translucent, just shy of transparent. Water trickled gently in tiny tributaries, over the edge of her nearly invisible bikini bottom, disappearing into the damp, dark, lovely triangle between her thighs. Cynthia found herself staring a little too hard. This was way past mere nudity . . . far more erotic. The kind of vision that she supposed would cause even the straightest of women and the gayest men shiver a bit. The only thing left to the imagination was how Stone could have possibly resisted her. Cynthia had to give him credit. Not succumbing to this girl's charms was a testament to the sincerity of the story he'd told her.

"You must be Cynthia," said the woman, extending her delicate hand to shake. Her gamine fingers were the kind that every girl wants and every man surely wants to be touched by. Breeding. Beauty. Intelligence. And a heaping helping of sensuality, the kind that is simultaneously classy and slutty. "We spoke on the phone. I'm Mariana."

"I know," said Cynthia, feeling a little uncomfortable, knowing what she now knew about her.

"Mariana, dear," said Stone, "you realize you're still fired, right?"

"Yup," she replied, padding across the tile floor and down the hall, presumably to put some clothes on. Presumably. Who knows, maybe this was as dressed as this girl ever got.

"Just wanted to get one more swim in."

"Look at that," said Jack, shaking his head in admiration. "That ass is a miracle."

"I've gotta hand it to you," said Cynthia, "Celebrity obsession aside, I admire your restraint."

"Yeah, well, her father is my producing partner. So, you know, don't give me too much credit."

"Well, that explains it," she said. "Let's get back to your warts."

"Yes, absolutely," he said, suddenly looking a little shy, like he might be about to spill secrets. He pulled open a large lazy Susan, spinning it slowly, revealing that it was stocked to the hilt with booze. "But maybe we should add a splash of Maker's Mark to our coffee."

"Umm . . . it's 10:15 A.M."

He glanced at the clock on the wall. "Hmm. So it is," he said, pouring more bourbon into his coffee than there was coffee. "But it's five o'clock somewhere. Maybe Paris." He counted the time difference in his head. "Maybe not. But who cares?"

"Certainly not me," said Cynthia, pushing her coffee cup in his direction.

Day 1, Chapter 2

Marjorie Amas used a variety of magnets——old cartoon character fast food giveaways from when her daughter was young, real estate calendar magnets, assorted plastic mini-fruits, and the like——to pin the Second Act headshots to her refrigerator. She made herself a third cup of tea and stepped back to consider the eight men Cynthia had chosen for her.

Her first reaction was that they were all too old. Of course they were all considerably younger than *she was*, but that was beside the point.

Let's see . . . Thomas Jordan, M.D. He has his own practice in Santa Monica. Not bad. He's got a nice smile. "Opera enthusiast?" Give me a break. I am not going to try to like opera again. I can't figure out what's even going on. And that date with that other opera buff was a nightmare. Two hours before the show spent on tutoring me in preparation. And for what? A story that could be summed up in three simple sentences: Man loves woman. Woman loves another. Everyone dies. Great. And then an hour in the car while the suitor sang the whole thing again, translating the Italian after every line. Fantastico. I've had it with opera nerds. I'd rather see a movie, have a good meal, and make some real off-stage passion.

She found a red pen in a kitchen drawer and drew a large "X" through Thomas Jordan's face. *So long, Pavarotti wannabe.*

Okay, Rupert Diamont. Entertainment lawyer. West L.A. "Cat lover." *Sorry, allergic.*

Big red "X."

Marjorie examined the stats and statements of every man on that Frigidaire, eventually crossing out all of them. She was tough. This was why she was alone. Of course, she blamed her daughter.

How could Cynthia even think I'd be vaguely interested in this bunch of losers? Doesn't she even know *me?*

She took them down, balled them up and deposited them into the recycling bin.

She sipped her tea and dialed Cynthia . . . who didn't pick up. *Great. She's hobnobbing with Hollywood royalty and sticks me with a stack of nincompoops.*

She glanced over at her computer. She sat down and turned it on. Cynthia didn't know it of course, but Marjorie was actually much more competent on the internet than she let on. She had delved into certain racy websites on her own. Not porn . . . she had typed in some sex-oriented keywords once and found herself bombarded with a cavalcade of obscene images that she was still trying to erase from her memory. No, she had gotten into the habit of seeking out tamer sensual stuff like photos of young athletes, especially swimmers, with their skimpy speedos and lean, muscular physiques. Margie's deceased husband had been a swimmer——"a champion breast stroker" he'd always joked——and she'd never really gotten over those broad shoulders. She had a thing for Olympian Michael Phelps. Downloading photos of him had become her secret hobby. She'd made a folder of them on the computer desktop. She had even gone to see him when he did a book signing at the Beverly Center. She'd printed a tall stack of pictures, waited in line, and then presented him with them all to be autographed. His handlers quickly insisted that the rule was one per customer, but Marjorie could tell that Michael himself would have been glad to oblige. He had looked at her with a sly smile and obvious recognition that they had something special together. He had touched her hand in a way that spoke volumes and she was absolutely positive that he would have signed each and every one of them if his moronic assistant hadn't ushered Marjorie out of the store, patting her on the back like she was some kind of demented super-fan . . . which she obviously was. Truth be told, she knew she was, but she was beyond caring how crazy she did or didn't look. Bottom line, her closet would be a veritable shrine, plastered with inscribed photos instead of merely being home to one: "To Margie—the lovely photograph lady! Sorry I couldn't sign them all! – Michael Phelps." In any case, it had been fun to meet him and she cherished the memory.

She found the Second Acts site, used her password to get into the site and went to the available men section. She scrolled through faces, so many which were handsomer and younger than the selection Cynthia had dropped off. Now this was what she was talking about. And then, one seemed to literally jump from the screen and kiss her on the lips, he was so appealing, so romantic looking, so damn hot.

Wow . . . Dominic Orlando. Now he has the kind of old-world look I love. And he's sixteen years younger than I am. Perfect: not too old, not too young. The kind of dark eyes you want to fall into and never come out. He also looks kind and sensitive. And somehow kind of innocent. And he works in a luxury hotel that could obviously have its advantages. And he likes to swim. Bingo.

Of course, Margie had totally misinterpreted Dominic's calculated romantic gaze in the photo as "innocent." She had no idea that he was a personal friend of Cynthia's or that he was one of the all-time great womanizers in Hollywood. He had so many notches, his belt had fallen to pieces, leaving nothing at all to hold his pants up. He was legendary and despite his epic reputation as a Lothario, women still loved him. He was a lovable letch. But Margie could only see the lovable part.

Now that's the guy I want to meet.

She called Cynthia again, and again, but she still didn't pick up. Cynthia was enjoying her second coffee with bourbon, poolside with a handsome movie star, who, try as he may to confess his faults, remained unconvincing.

Marjorie left her daughter a message: "Hi, honey. I found someone I'm interested in and I'll check his box on the site. Have a nice day and say hello to Mr. Stone for me. He knows me. Remember? I once took a picture of him on the patio at The Ivy Restaurant? My camera bumped his martini, which spilled all over his shirt. Even though he insisted he could handle it, I'm sure he appreciated me helping to clean him up. And interrupting that boring business meeting he was having with his agent and some grumpy producer . . . that had to be a welcome break from those stuffed shirts. Also, do you think he might sign a few photographs for me? Maybe ask him? Okay, then, that's all. So, let me know when I can see the man I chose. I'm kind of anxious to set up something. Okay, now I'm talking too long. Okay, I really should hang up now because . . ."

BEEEEEEEP! You have exceeded the time allotted for your message. If you would like to listen to your message, press one. If you would like to record a new message, press two. For other options, press 3.

Margie wondered what the other options were, but decided to let the original message stand, and hung up. But then she called back. "Hi, honey. It's Mom again. I just wanted to say goodbye properly. So, goodbye, and give me a call when you get this. Even though I know you won't. You never return my calls. So why do I even *leave* them? Why even *have* voicemail if you're not even going to call people back? Or is it just me you don't call back? Anyway . . . oh, did you know that Pete Blatt is back in town . . . and he's still single? I just heard from my friend Martha that she heard from her friend Sally, that somebody she knows bumped into him on Ventura Boulevard and that he's single."

BEEEEEEEP!

Day 1, Chapter 3

After four cups of bourbon-laden coffee, Cynthia was a little jittery *and* dizzy——that speedy-blurry electric buzz. They had moved into the sunken living room overlooking the pool and the rest of the universe, and she had slipped deep into the soft leather couch. It was *too* soft, really . . . the kind of sofa that, if you actually *tried* to sit up straight, you'd end up with a backache. It was far better to surrender to its recesses and lay there like you were ready to nap, or be sexually violated, or both. The view, the relaxed opulence, the whole thing, was pretty much heaven.

"And so," said Jack Stone, now on his umpteenth anecdote that, although purportedly divulged to highlight his faults, only magnified his devastating appeal, "that was how *that* ended. Sure, she is a fabulous actress and a so-called sex symbol, but she's really kind of soulless compared to you . . .

and certainly not as beautiful."

Cynthia rolled her eyes and blushed again, wondering which starlet he was talking about *now*. But suddenly she realized her bladder was very full.

"Thanks, Jack. By the way, does this dump have indoor plumbing?" It amazed her that somehow she'd reached this very familiar place with Stone. He got her sense of humor and she didn't hold back.

"No," he laughed, gesturing with a nod toward a hallway lined with art that looked suspiciously like original cubist collages, "but there's a very nice 'Johnny on the Spot' right through there."

"Are those what I think they are?" she queried, squinting and pulling herself up high enough over the back of the couch to get a better look, then gasping slightly.

"If you're thinking three Picassos, two Braques, and one Gris . . . yes," he said. "Gifts from my agent. I'm thinking about re-gifting, though. I'm not that into Cubism. You want one? I gave a Matisse *painting* to my friend Will Ferrell recently. Not because I like him so much——I was just sick of looking at that green-and-purple-faced old woman. I bet he's pawned it off on someone else by now."

Jesus. It must be strange to be so rich that nothing is irreplaceable. Some wealthy people are married to possessions. Stone seemed like he'd be perfectly happy to bulldoze the place and start over at the drop of a hat.

"Oh, well," she said. "I would have taken the *Matisse* off your hands."

"Too bad," he said, smiling again, this time with a hint of impishness, an unmistakable trace of innuendo. "Maybe there's something *else* I can give you."

Cynthia felt herself blush. *Wow.* She was getting the distinct impression that he liked her. Whatever fine line separated joviality and desire seemed to have been crossed.

This was kind of a dream come true, but possibly a nightmare, career-wise. She wanted his business and the word of mouth that would flow if he found Second Acts worth recommending to his fellow A-listers. Plus, she wasn't stupid or drunk enough to believe that she was *that* special. Stone was clearly a pick-up artist, whether he thought of himself like that or not. One way or another, he'd left an endless trail of bewitched, bothered, and bewildered beauties in his wake without even breaking a sweat. Cynthia realized that even in the best possible version of this fantasy——at its most deluded and fairy tale-like——how long could it actually last?

But good god, he is sexy. I have the distinct impression that if I simply reach out and touch his hand or shoulder or smile a slightly suggestive smile, we would spend the rest of the day rolling around his bedroom. Or deep within the quicksand of this couch. But no, I will resist him. The byword is "professional." If there's one thing I've learned it's that business and pleasure don't mix. Like oil and water. But unfortunately, oil is incredibly beautiful when it's floating on water. The way the light catches it. Dazzling. Intoxicating as a matter of fact. They don't mention that when they're dishing out clichés in the cliché line at the ol' cliché cafeteria. What am I talking about? Now her bladder was about to explode. "Oh, okay. To the ladies' room it is," she smiled, lifting the cup to her lips for one last sip. She realized she had already taken the last sip a moment earlier——there was nothing there. Thankfully. But she pantomimed finishing it off anyway. "God, that's good," she said, smacking her lips and wondering if he noticed she was drinking air.

She stood up and, although she wasn't *terribly* tipsy, she was certainly more so than usual for a weekday morning. As she moved toward the hallway, she remembered another daytime drinking episode. The memory fluttered into her mind like a sexually charged butterfly, distracting her and obliterating any interest she might have had in the priceless artworks she was passing . . . a memory named Pete Blatt. She couldn't believe it: Pete Blatt again.

Cynthia had gone to high school with Pete and they'd

fooled around once. She had come to think of it as the Pisco Pete Incident. It involved the aforementioned potent Peruvian libation, a large bag of Cheetos, and a fun, drunken swirl of messy sexual exploration.

Cynthia had thought about a lot of her first boyfriends lately, but especially Pete. He was incredibly quiet, but cute, talented, and so in love with her. Maybe more so than anyone ever. She wondered if that were actually true. She considered it and decided that it probably was. She wondered what he had turned into. It had taken her years to realize how deeply that afternoon of erotic fumbling was etched into her heart. She instantly saw the sunlight filtered through her childhood curtains, smelled the Cheetos, tasted the Pisco on Pete's lips and the sweat on his skin. Sitting with him there on her bed, the bed she'd been tucked into every night by her parents when she was little, was so wrong and so right. Even now it was crystal clear in her mind's eye: their absurdly skinny, angular bodies, covered in peach fuzz; the tan line— —something you barely see anymore——that described her hip and belly and bottom and back and blossoming breasts like a bright white bikini. It was erotic to *her*, god knows it must have driven *him* insane; the freckles around his nose; his nervous sexual yearning . . . from those beyond blue eyes, to his flushed cheeks, to his twitching, twanging erection.

Such innocence, such desperation——like an adolescent opera——like they were sharing an exotic, illicit drug. Utterly intoxicating. It was funny and sexy and bigger than life usually gets.

She remembered something she'd totally forgotten. When she'd first taken off her top, he'd gasped and couldn't speak. He'd tried but was literally rendered mute. He'd reached out, his hands trembling, her flesh waiting. She remembered his fingertips were calloused from playing the guitar and that he'd been concerned that they'd be too rough. Unable to form the words, he'd pantomimed it. She'd appreciated the sweetness of that. She'd whispered, "Maybe you should kiss them instead. You know——if you want to." His eyes widened and he nodded like some kind of adorable, sex-crazed zombie. He moved in, first tentatively, gingerly tasting her right nipple with the tip of his tongue, like he was afraid it might be poison, like this whole thing was some crazy trap he'd been lured into. But then he licked it like a lollipop——watching in awe as it reacted——and finally took it all in, devouring it like a hungry man or a starving baby. Or both. He was ravenous. He placed one of his hands on her left breast, like he was just holding it there so it couldn't get away, letting his other arm dangle at his side. She lifted that hand, placed it on her lap, pushed it between her legs, and squeezed her thighs together. Two tidal waves of warmth——one emanating from her chest, the other from below——merged. She felt like she was melting inside. She placed her other hand on his knee and slowly traveled upward, grabbing on like a joystick in a video arcade. It was hot and hard and fantastic.

It exploded.

And then Pete threw up.

In retrospect, not all that satisfying, of course, but still, when it came to the mysterious, electrifying, otherworldly thrill that kind of brand-spanking newness provided, nothing in grown-up life came close. Strange that she was thinking about him now. Why in traffic earlier? Why here, in the house of this major movie star? Weird.

And that was why, when she checked her voicemail while anointing Jack Stone's unbelievably beautiful powder room——after first being driven up a wall by most of her mother's rambling——she was truly flabbergasted by fourteen simple words embedded within that verbal wasteland: *Did you know that Pete Blatt is back in town . . . and that he's single?*

What? You've got to be kidding. What kind of crazy coincidence is that? What did he even look like now?

She imagined two versions: fat Pete versus fit Pete. *Which way had he gone? She'd heard he'd moved to the Midwest—— maybe Wisconsin?——at one point. What had he done with his life? What did he do for a living? And are we talking single-single or divorced-single? Are there dozens of Pete and Patricia Juniors running around? Not that it matters that much. Just wondering.*

Bzzzz. Cynthia looked down at her phone: Lolita. *What the hell, I'll pick up.*

"Just checking up on me, Lo? Jesus, you're worse than my mother."

"Damn straight. I'm *way* worse than your mother. Okay, I need an update. Are you still there?"

"As a matter of fact, I'm in his bathroom at this very moment."

"No way. You are perched upon Jack Stone's throne? That is awesome. Please, do something for me: don't ever wash that bottom. Good god, can you at least grab me a souvenir? A washcloth or a guest towel or something?"

"Lolita," she whispered, turning on the tap and picking up a luxurious bar of soap that looked like it had been handcrafted by angels, "I don't really think burglary is the recommended course of action while cultivating client relations. My god, this soap smells good."

"Come on! At least tell me how it's going."

"Oh, it's going fine." She lifted her sudsy hands to her face. "This soap is divine."

"Cynthia! Enough with the soap! *Give* me something.

Details. *Something.* I'm sitting here surrounded by dogs and covered with fur. Throw me a freaking bone. What is he looking for in a girl? Give me a list of requirements. I'll dye my hair. I'll change my personality. I'll shave, bleach, or rejuvenate *anything.* Breast surgery——augmentation *or* reduction——is not out of the question."

"Calm down, Lolita. He actually seems like a really normal guy. We're sort of hitting it off. I kinda like 'im." She sort of slurred that last part--the bourbon had infiltrated her consonants.

"Cynthia, have you been drinking? Are you nuts? What do you mean you *kind of like him?* How can you *kind of like* Jack Stone? He's *Jack freaking Stone.*"

"I don't know," she said, now a little defensive about the drinking comment and also about how she was supposed to be so in awe of a movie star. Granted, he was wonderful in person, but Lolita didn't know that. "It's weird, but I think he likes *me.*"

That stopped Lolita in her tracks. Cynthia thought the call had dropped.

"Hello? Lolita? Did you hear what I said? I think he might actually *like* me."

"I heard you the first time!" she exclaimed, clearly irritated. "I don't think that's remotely possible, but, yes I did hear you."

"Oh, really?" Now Cynthia was pissed.

"Don't take it so personally, Miss Amas. I think you just might be slightly deluded, that's all. It would be easy for that to happen . . . you know, being with someone like that. It could kind of go to your head. But mostly I'm wondering. Aren't you supposed to be looking for a match for *me*, after all?"

"Oh, Lolita, dear?" she said in the sweetest voice she could muster under the circumstances.

"Yes, Cynthia, dear?"

Cynthia didn't actually know what she wanted to do about Jack Stone yet. She was pretty confident she could have him if she wanted to . . . at least for the afternoon. Beyond that, she wasn't so sure. In any case, although she obviously didn't know him that well, she was quite sure that Lolita was exactly what he *wasn't* looking for.

She waited a beat, then quietly, but firmly, said, "I'm sure I can find someone for you too, Lo. But, for now, I'd better get back to my *Jack*. So long. This. Conversation. Is. Over." She hung up, switched off her phone, and laughed, covering her mouth with her fingers.

Cynthia dried her hands and inspected herself in the mirror. She reapplied lip-gloss. She leaned in closer to her reflection. She remembered the scene in *Five Easy Pieces*, when Jack Nicholson, on a highway to nowhere, gazes introspectively into a gas station restroom mirror. He looks hard at himself. At first he studies his features, seemingly struggling to recognize the man staring back at him. But then he peers past the surface into his brain and down deeper into his heart and soul——and makes a decision.

Cynthia also made a decision. In terms of jeopardizing her life and livelihood, freefalling into Stone's arms would be way more destructive than even her on-again, off-again hot fling with Max, her longtime, maddeningly addictive sometime lover. Stone was like Max on fame steroids. She could totally imagine spending four or five divine hours or days in Jack's bed, but once his urge to merge subsided, she'd likely be dumped down an emotional laundry chute before sunrise.

It's so odd, but sometimes you actually require a mirror. You need to literally look at yourself.

She'd found that to be true so many times. She consulted with mirrors like some people read horoscopes. When her marriage was crashing and burning it was her conversation with her reflection that clarified life. Same with the decision to drop out of the corporate studio world and start Second Acts in the first place. A mirror the restroom of the Standard Hotel told her everything she needed to know.

She returned to the living room, but Jack Stone was gone. Then she heard the diving board and looked up to see his body in midair, tight charcoal grey swimsuit, arcing up——a picture-perfect display of bona fide screen-idol magic—— and over, plunging deep into the blue. She moved through the sliding doors and onto the patio, walking to the far end of the pool.

Stone emerged, planted his palms, and lifted himself effortlessly to a posture-perfect standing position——suddenly right there, close, the pool-reflected sunlight dancing on his sculpted physique. What had seemed like a movie-magazine photo spread during the dive had now materialized by her side in the flesh.

He leaned over, lifted a towel off a chaise, and dried himself. He looked into her eyes and tenderly touched her face with his fingertips, following eyebrow, to cheekbone, to jaw, to chin, to lips.

Cynthia couldn't help it. She did what any red-blooded girl would do. She kissed his hand.

"Cynthia," he said in a tone that was not overtly seductive, just low and matter-of-fact, like he was saying something obvious, something she would clearly agree with, "I have a feeling we don't need your dating service to find each other." The corner of his mouth turned up just slightly, as if to say *I'm serious, I mean this, I want you.*

She was surprised how much it made her shiver, because

as unlikely and dreamlike this turn of events would have seemed a couple of hours ago, *now* was a whole other story. She had been expecting it. But no matter how much you see it coming, when someone like Jack Stone makes a move on you, it bothers you to your core. She felt his touch simultaneously on her skin and deep within like he had perfected some kind of sensual sonar. This was not merely a gorgeous man. This was a gorgeous man plus an entire fantasy-fueled catalog of films and characters and romanticized narratives. It was bearing down on her . . . a delirious dream magnified exponentially by the awesome power of the big screen. She hadn't forgotten the silly rumor about his *size* either. In fact, presently, as he moved close, wrapping his arms around her and completely eliminating the space between their bodies, his wet suit barely contained his growing enthusiasm and it didn't feel silly at all. It felt very real. His heat had already taken the chill out of the suit. The rumor was no rumor. She thought of Lolita, who had said, in reference to her fling with Maximillian Schell, "Until you've tried it, you can never know just how good it feels to get made love to by a big movie star in a big beautiful mansion on a hill." Well, here he was. She felt the blood in her cheeks. She knew they were burning bright. Her skin, her lips, her entire body was straining against the decision her mind had already made.

"Jack," she said softly in his ear, "I'm flattered. I mean *very* flattered. And I'm really sorry. Sorry I kissed your hand or did anything else to lead you on. I like you. I can totally imagine falling for you. Falling *hard* for you. In fact, at the moment I'm feverish from head to toe. In a good way. But I'm involved with someone else and I simply cannot do this to him." This was of course a lie. Even as she said it, she doubted her sanity. Who in her right mind says no to Jack Stone, to this particular here and now? Cynthia Amas, apparently.

Stone released and backed away slightly, just far enough to look into her eyes.

"Wow," he said, smiling sweetly, not offended, or at least hiding it well. "Refreshing. I was not expecting that. No problem, though. If things change, let me know. That is one lucky man you've got."

One lucky man. Right. She was of course referring to Pete Blatt, someone she hadn't seen in twenty years, who, for all she knew, could have a beer belly the size of Milwaukee. But more than that she was considering the impact on Second Acts. She really didn't want to risk everything for a fling that was undoubtedly destined to be short-lived. After all, despite her uncanny gifts as a love conjurer for others, even under normal circumstances her own love life was cursed.

"Okay, I'll do that," she said. But she was so taken by his

simple, confident, un-pushy response to her rejection——
something he had possibly never experienced in his entire
life——that she almost wanted to blurt out that somehow,
miraculously, things had *already* changed, as in *Did I say I was
seeing someone? Because what I meant to say was——hello—
—I am so not seeing anyone. So please, Mr. Movie Star, ravage
me now. I'm ready. I'm on fire. A six-alarm fire. I'm yours.*

But she didn't. *Remember. Focus. The business, the business.*

"I'm really sorry, Jack, I need to get going. I have another
appointment. But I'm absolutely positive that I can find
someone for you who you'll like a whole lot more than little
old me."

"I'm dubious, but thanks," he said. "Let me know what the
next step is. My office will send over a check."

"Oh," she said. "They already did. Thanks for that." And
she meant it. He'd bought ten successive, deluxe packages.
This was far more than he needed, especially if he was
actually planning on "settling down." But his office said
it was more about supporting a local business, so who was
Cynthia to argue?

They walked side-by-side through the house and up the
driveway, all the way to her car. She swung the door open,
preparing for the final goodbye. He touched her shoulder . . .
sort of squeezing, sort of caressing. Slow and warm and firm.

Perfect. As he slid his hand downward along her bicep, his thumb brushed the outside of her breast, causing yet another delicious shudder that again almost made her reconsider everything . . . possibly her entire life.

This is a siren song and I am Odysseus. I could live in that house. I could re-gift famous works of art with the best of them. Why work? This could be my Bel Air super-hunk-movie-star-hideaway. Why not? Somebody's gotta do it. No. The business, the business, resist, resist.

"I can't tell you how nice it was to meet you," he said. "One of the best Thursday morning meetings ever. Short, sweet, and profound. And to think it could have been even better. But no matter . . . you are exactly what the doctor ordered: a lovely prescription for what was ailing me. Even if the dosage was way too low." He smiled, knowing the metaphor was silly--but true and sincere.

She smiled too. She tasted the Maker's Mark in her throat and the words she'd said to herself earlier returned. She repeated them several times to herself like two competing mantras: *Please ravage me now. No, the business. I'm ready. I'm yours. No, the business.*

She slid onto the car seat, turned the key, and pulled away, carving a large U-turn in his enormous driveway, saying, with a mixture of fortitude and regret, "Jack," (*Good god, I can't believe I'm even calling him Jack, much less turning him down),* "we'll talk soon."

Jack Stone waved goodbye. He stood there in his perfect swimsuit, in his perfect driveway, on his perfect piece of property . . . perfectly perplexed. Not one single female had rejected him since his acne had cleared up in the ninth grade. Why her, why now?

Scarlett O'Hara padded up behind him and stuck her cold nose into the back of his knee, deliberately, like this was where it belonged, like a ship coming home to dock. This startled him, making him flinch slightly. He reached down and scratched the dog's head and behind her ear. Together they watched Cynthia's convertible wind its way up the long drive and out onto the street, disappearing behind an enormous jasmine bush, the sound of her engine revving and humming and fading away. "Between you and me," he said to his furry friend, "this is not over. I'm serious. I mean this. I want her. I must have her."

Day 1, Chapter 4

Lolita's high-end Beverly Hills dog grooming shop was bustling to say the least. She was dealing with five customers with nine dogs in the front and Tanya, her young assistant, had a full house in the back. Lolita was preoccupied with the whole Cynthia-Jack situation and resented the fact that, even though she was the one who had made the Stone connection through the dogs, Cynthia was receiving all the benefits . . . and the benefits seemed really, really good. As in steamy A.M. sex and possibly P.M. *love*. With. Jack. Stone.

The current congregation of canines in the cutting room sensed they were not receiving anyone's full attention and were demanding it rather forcefully. Barks and whines and growls were at a high decibel level.

"Tanya!" Lolita called to her young assistant. "Put some soothing music on! Anything classical. Except no *Wagner!*

That'll push them totally over the edge! Bach: good. Mozart: better. Brahms: best!"

This got a laugh from a few of the customers, which calmed Lolita a bit. But unbeknownst to her, Tanya's new boyfriend, a hip-hop artist (part rapper, part dancer, part electronic-funk genius) named Dr. T-Bone, who worked early nights on the Third Street Promenade in Santa Monica and late nights, sometimes all night, in the clubs, had dropped in through the back door of the shop to pay Tanya a visit. Their opposite schedules weren't terribly conducive to intimate activity and they had both reached a fever pitch of sexual frustration, catching a kiss and a hug here and there on the fly, but not much else. At that very moment, Tanya's metallic miniskirt was wriggling up and her boyfriend's baggy pants were slipping even further down than usual.

When, after a few long minutes of waiting——the dogs still causing an alarming cacophony——with absolutely zero strains of classical anything wafting her way, Lolita had had enough.

"Tanya!" she screamed, quite a bit more loudly and shrilly than one expects in front of customers in a tony shop in a neighborhood like this.

"Just a minute!" screeched Tanya, a strange desperation in her voice, like she was in trouble, like she'd gotten hurt or something. Lolita had once cut herself while clipping an uncooperative Daschund and she immediately jumped to conclusions.

"Oh, my god, will you excuse me?" she said as politely as possible to the matronly woman with three extremely unruly Toy Yorkies, doing their best to terrorize an absurdly patient ancient Saint Bernard, who may or may not have been deaf and blind. "I have to check on something."

"Tanya!" she said, pushing open the swinging doors. "Are you okay?!"

But what she saw stopped her dead in her tracks. It wasn't just that Tanya's tank top was hiked high above her tiny, perfect, jiggling breasts and her legs were wrapped tightly around T-Bone, as he pounded mercilessly away, chanting *baby, baby, baby* . . . although it all did seem a tad inappropriate for the workplace. And it wasn't just that they were doing it on top of one of the cutting tables and fur was floating in the air like snowflakes in a snow globe. Or that all those dogs——including her beloved King, Max, and Wilfredo——were being exposed to this kind of behavior, potentially scarring them for life. Lolita knew a thing or two about dog psychology, thank you very much. It wasn't merely that she was paying her sexy young assistant twenty dollars an hour for one service and the girl was providing quite another for

Dr. Slick T-Bone on her dime. No, it was also incredibly annoying to Lolita that apparently the whole world was having scorching-hot sex this morning, except her. She, of course, wrongfully assumed that Cynthia was currently consummating things with Jack Stone and she was having great difficulty not being deeply bothered by that. She tried to convince herself that she didn't care. She loved Cynthia and wanted her to be happy, after all. But she was also aggravated. When it came right down to it, this was part of who she was. She had been deeply competitive her whole life, especially when it came to men. She'd lost friends over this kind of thing. She had fallen for married men several times and broken up at least two marriages. She wasn't proud of it——she'd seen a therapist about it. She didn't even think she'd have much of a chance with Jack Stone, it was just that she wanted Cynthia to try to make it happen for her, as a friend. Instead, *this*? After all her talk about her old fling with Maximillian Schell, she felt like Cynthia had trumped her without even trying. Her favorite Hollywood brush with fame had lost much of its luster in comparison to the first class fame-brushing going down in Bel Air at that very moment.

Tanya was history anyway, but everything else intensified Lolita's multi-layered feeling of betrayal. Tanya bore the brunt of it all.

"Get out," she shrieked. "Get out *now*! I invested a lot of time and money training you, Tanya. And this is what I get?!"

"But Lolita," she cried, pulling down her skirt, wriggling her top back over her breasts, "remember, I walked in on you with that actor that time. How is that different? I didn't freak out. I thought it was kind of funny! I was *happy* for you, remember? T-Bone and I *love* each other, but we can never seem to find time to *make* love to each other!"

That was it for Lolita. "Aren't you sweet. You're in love," she mocked in a super syrupy tone. "Tanya, you want to know how it's different? The difference *is this is my shop!* I can fuck anyone I want back here! If you want to get boned by your precious T-Bone in a dog grooming shop, you'll need to start your own! Meanwhile, you'll have plenty of time for screwing whomever you want *whenever* you want, because you're fired!"

"But Lolita!" cried Tanya, struggling to thread her army boots through the tiny leg holes of her pink leopard-patterned panties.

"GET THE HELL OUT!" shrieked Lolita so emphatically that that there was no point in responding in any way other than just getting the hell out.

Tanya and T-Bone exited quickly through the back, both partially dressed. Tanya was crying, but T-Bone was more concerned about where they could go now to finish what they had started. "Is your mother home now, baby?" "I just lost my job, T-Bone!" "I know, I know . . . it's BAD. Really terrible. But really, do you think your mom's out?"

Lolita slammed the back door and comforted all the dogs a bit.

"King, sweetie, just block that whole thing out. Breathe. Picture a ball on a beach. And Max, don't let this horrible experience close your mind to all men everywhere. Mommy would never do anything like that in front of you. You know that." She turned to Wilfredo, the little one.

"Wilfredo, can you forgive me?"

The tiny Chihuahua gazed into her imploring blue eyes with his watery black ones and said, just as clear as day, to Lolita at least, "We've discussed this and have come to the conclusion that there are good and bad men. Good ones throw the ball more than once. They know when to scratch behind ears and when to rub bellies. They let you sniff and lick their hand. They don't pull back and complain and wipe it off in disgust. We talked this all over with Scarlett O'Hara, that Wheaten, and although we haven't had the pleasure of meeting him, we believe her master, Master Jack, is a good one. A very good one. Undoubtedly the man for you. Your romantic destiny. And here is that kid's wallet."

Sure enough, Wilfredo had slipped T-Bone's wallet from his pants while T-Bone was getting into Tanya's.

"Wilfredo," she said, holding his tiny head in her hands and glaring at him like an angry mother, "I am so tired of returning this stuff. Please cut it out." Then she softened. "But very good work on the Scarlet O'Hara/Jack Stone front. She kissed him full on the lips. She fished her cell phone out of her pocket and called Cynthia.

The phone rang and rang and rang.

Day 1, Chapter 5

Cynthia was driving along Sunset, crossing La Cienega, heading toward Chateau Marmont to have coffee with her friend Dominic Orlando——a dedicated bachelor, *very* dedicated——who had recently signed up for Second Acts Dating Service. She was dubious, but supportive.

She looked down and saw who was making her phone ring. She knew what Lolita thought she and Jack Stone were in the middle of doing in his house, in his bed. She decided to ignore the phone and let her think that. She didn't want to have to deal with telling Lolita that Jack Stone would not be interested in her.

She had a couple of phone calls to make herself.

Ringing.

"Hello, Cynthia! How are you, darling?"

This was Diego, Cynthia's good friend who'd barely

survived a nightmare of a date with Lolita. She really wanted to find him someone as special as he was. He'd gotten his PhD in Semiotics from Berkeley ten years earlier and was now teaching at Occidental. But he was no dry egghead. He had sold a screenplay last year——a comedy——and was working on another now. He was also a single-panel cartoonist and had been published in lots of magazines. And a skydiver. And a gourmet cook. He spoke four languages that she knew of. And he was a really nice guy. The guy was a catch and truly an adventurous soul when it came to women . . . up for almost anything. He wisely drew the line at dates——no matter how good their architecturally miraculous breasts looked in topless lederhosen——who come chaperoned by jealous, bloodthirsty, two-hundred-pound-plus canines, thank you very much, Lolita. Cynthia really hoped she'd found someone just right for him now.

"So, Diego, are you good with my selection? She is one spectacular lady . . . little, cute, and tight, like you like. As I said in the email, she was a statewide gymnastics champ. She went to the Olympics one year. She was robbed of a medal."

"So, what exactly happened?"

"Well, she had just turned eighteen and was feeling pretty elated about reaching the age of consent. A huge Swedish track star came on strong to her the night before her qualifying round, and she went for it. How could she know he was sixteen? She thought he was in his twenties. He certainly looked like it at six feet four; I mean, she came up to about his waist. It never occurred to her in a million years that she could ever be robbing a cradle."

"Oh, wow. Reverse jailbait."

"Yeah, anyway, it really derailed her Olympic career and got her thinking about other paths, which eventually led to law school and all the rest. She's an entertainment attorney, so she might be a great asset for you in that way too. But she is still a gymnast at heart. She's thirty-three, but looks ten years younger. She's whip-smart, super athletic, hot girlie sexy, and light as a feather. You do the math. I mean, if you're into that."

"Cynthia, stop talking! I'm driving."

"Sorry, Diego, I'm just picturing the two of you having a really good time. You with your tremendous upper-body strength, she with her, oh I don't know, *maneuverability?*"

"Cynthia!"

"Okay, sounds like you're all set. Call me with any questions. Like, Cynthia, does Costco sell condoms in bulk?"

"Cynthia!"

"Okay, bye, sweetie!" she laughed, pulling up the long, steep driveway of one of the most famous hotel on the west coast, Chateau Marmont.

The valet took her keys and smiled. "How are you today, Madame?"

"Very well, thanks. And you?"

"I could not be better."

Cynthia loved cheerfulness like that. This guy was standing in front of a hotel all day long, catering to all kinds of celebrities and other over-privileged brats, yet he sounded like he was on a beach somewhere relaxed, cheerful, and gracious. She tipped him well. She wanted to encourage relaxed, cheerful, and gracious whenever she could.

She made her way to the lobby, along the way noticing three or four familiar faces of hot, young up-and-comers whose names eluded her. A wrinkly guy was holding court on one of the couches. He looked like a much older version of James Caan, but then she realized it *was* James Caan and he was just a lot older. She preferred him frozen in time as Sonny, the hot and hotheaded Corleone brother mowed down in the first *Godfather*, not this distinguished grandpa.

"Cynthia, my darling little Putenesca!" boomed a voice behind her, the incredible Dominic Orlando.

"Dominic," she gushed, truly happy to see him. She had had a crush on him a while back, but it abruptly stopped when she realized just how many women felt the same way.

There had been———as he was prone to call it———a revolving dessert case of tiramisu wherever he and his famous cannoli went. It was before the idea of sex *addiction* had really caught on, but that was definitely what he was "suffering" from. He almost lost his job at Chateau Marmont more than once.

The most recent episode involved an Eastern European super model, the wife of an English Shakespearean actor, who, while her husband was shooting a well-known, high-budget, very dumb science fiction movie———long, frustrating hours speaking leaden dialogue to invisible aliens against miles of green screen———was spending many of those same hours playing hide the salami with everyone's favorite Sicilian Stallion.

What happened in Marmont would have stayed in Marmont if the super model hadn't given Dominic a very expensive and distinctive gold ring that her husband had presented her with when he'd signed on to the movie. It bore a large kunzite stone, chosen of course for its pale pink color and appropriately suggestive name, since it was intricately engraved to depict the folds of her labia. He'd called it his *signing boner*. Three days into their stay at the hotel, she fell hard for Dominic and wanted him to wear it on a chain around his neck, under his shirt, next to his skin, to remind him of her. He, afraid to be caught with it, but too much of a romantic to simply throw it away, gave it to a beautiful young bit player he wanted to bed . . . and then immediately did, unaware that she had just scored a small role on the very same science fiction movie.

During one long, hot and sweaty green-screen marathon, the ring, slightly too large for this particularly slender actress's finger, slipped off and rolled about twenty feet downstage, finally circling and resting at the feet of the cuckolded actor, who was inhaling lunch at the craft services table. He gagged on his iced coffee and passed out, landing in the potato salad. When he came to, he immediately accused the starlet of stealing it. When she denied it, the actor called his wife. She confirmed, that, yes, it must have been stolen. But when the husband explained to her how it had slipped off the finger of a stunning young actress, you know, the one with the nude scene everyone's talking about, she screamed bloody murder and the whole thing unraveled very quickly after that.

The craft services girl who witnessed this revelation immediately burst into tears, confessing that she too was in love with Dominic and that he had begged and begged and finally convinced her to participate in a three-way with the actor's wife the day before.

"I love him!" she screamed, attacking the actress with a large ladle that happened to be full of vegetable noodle soup at the time. "He's going to marry me! I'm his little Tiramisu!"

The capper was that just then, the assistant director on the film, a French woman in her fifties, walked in and, after removing a noodle from her hair, said, "That's funny, I had a boyfriend back in the early '90s——a costume designer—— who called me that. He was going to marry me too! What was his name again? Dominic something. Dominic *Orlando*!"

While all this was going on, Dominic was back at the hotel in a broom closet with a hot new young hotel housekeeper who had been hired by the hotel operations director literally minutes earlier.

Dominic and the housekeeper got fired. But as soon as that particular science fiction movie wrapped——eight days later——Dominic was re-hired. Nobody worked the concierge desk like Orlando. But they had him on a much tighter leash.

Which was why he signed up for Second Acts.

"Cynthia, Cynthia, Cynthia," he murmured, taking her hand in his and kissing her knuckles one at a time. "How I have missed you. I wouldn't need a dating service if you were ready to settle down."

This was of course hilarious coming from him.

"Settle down?" she asked, rolling her eyes. "You'll settle down when you're dead. Even then, I'm not so sure. The first cute young angel who flies by in a short tight robe . . ."

"Ha, ha. So funny," he interrupted, kissing her cheeks. "It is *you* who is my bellisimo angelo! But no, bella donna, that was the *old* me. I've changed. I had to. Next time I screw around, I'm out the door faster than you can say come to me my sweet little biscotti. Not to mention that eventually one of these husbands or boyfriends is gonna be packing heat. I'm getting too old for hiding under beds and shimmying down fire escapes. Boy do I have stories." He pointed downward, smiled mischievously, and continued, "Me and Senor Pepperoni have had a good run. Noi abbiamo assaggiato molto micio. But it's time. Time to find my true love——the whole kit and cannoli."

"Okay, okay, I get what you're saying," said Cynthia, taking his hand and leading him to the couch. She sat across from him in a large stuffed chair. "Except for that 'Noi abbiamo . . .' blah, blah, blah . . . what was that, pray tell?"

"Oh, yes, sorry. That's *we* . . . I was talking about me and, you know, my pepperoni. It's a sausage, but it kind of looks like . . ."

Cynthia shook her head. "Dominic, I know what a pepperoni is and what it looks like. I don't speak Italian, but I'm not an idiot."

"Oh, okay, sorry. So what I was saying was that me and

Mr. Pepperoni have tasted a lot of micio, you know . . . a lot of *cat*."

She rolled her eyes. "You mean pussy?"

"That's it! Yes, pussy . . . sesso!" he cheered, clapping his hands and kissing her cheeks again.

"Okay, okay," she said, "please, no more smooching——at least for the next two or three minutes. What are you looking for in a date? What have all your years of experience——not just with the *sesso*, mind you, but with the women *attached* to the sesso——taught you? What is your idea of a perfect mate?"

"Il mio dio! Good question, Cynthia. That's a tough one. You know, I think I love *all* women. Young, old, skinny, fat. They *all* appeal to me. I really don't enjoy the company of men so much. They don't smell so good."

"Okay, Dominic," said Cynthia, with mock seriousness, jotting down an invisible note with an imaginary pen. "Men . . . are . . . not . . . women. Got it."

"Okay, Cynthia," he said, flashing the smile that had charmed his way past more zippers, snaps, buttons, and hooks than there are stars in the heavens. "You're making fun of me now, but I don't care. I used to think I liked redheads the best, then, for a stretch it was all black all the time. Now I don't know. Lately the Asian ladies have been looking really, really good, you know? Seriously, I think I was put on this Earth to love them all."

"Hold on, Casanova," she said, starting to wonder if this entire meeting was a gigantic waste of time. She was very close to just standing up and walking out. "Are you serious about finding someone special or not?"

Dominic got quiet. His face drooped. He had a huge helping of thespian in him. All of a sudden an exaggerated expression of despair had transformed his face into a tragedy mask.

"Cynthia, darling, I have never been more serious about anything in my life. I need help. I admit that. We are friends. I am here for you and you for me. Help me help myself. I don't want to chase all the girls no more. I promise. Tell me what to do. Mi liberi. How do you say? *Rescue me.* Please, this is all I ask. *Rescue me.*"

Just then, two young party girls entered the lobby. They were well outside Dominic's peripheral vision, but Cynthia could tell from his not-so-subtle flinch that he had heard them come in. The tapping of their tiny spike heels, the carefree, anything-goes quality in their whispers and giggles. His ears didn't literally stand up like a dog's, but almost. The girls click-clacked their way to the center of the room, stopping to talk to each other a mere ten feet behind Dominic's head. But he didn't turn around. Cynthia knew he was trying to prove that his skirt-chasing days were over.

"Cynthia, go ahead," leaning in and whispering in a deadpan. "Describe them to me. I don't need to look. I don't even *want* to look."

"Right, Dominic. Okay, well, one of the girls is sporting the tiniest and tightest black miniskirt I have ever seen outside a strip club. It barely covers her underwear, assuming she's actually wearing any."

Dominic did not turn his head. He would not look.

Cynthia continued. "I mean, Dom, it might actually be one of those tube-top bras that she has simply shimmied down around her ass. Then up on top is a fake fur cape . . . fuchsia. Il mio dio, that looks soft. It's just sort of hovering above her otherwise nude, gravity-defying breasts like a strawberry cloud. The slightest breeze would blow it away."

"This is supposed to be interesting to me, I am guessing?" asked Dominic, his eyes vibrating slightly, his heart palpitating, but somehow still staring straight ahead.

"And the other girl," Cynthia continued, "good heavens, her pants are tight. If it's any indication, her camel toe is so prominent, I'm not completely sure the pants are even pants. They might be sprayed on."

"Thank you, Cynthia," he said, "but this is of no concern to the new Orlando."

Cynthia was impressed with his restraint. She had to hand it to him, he was serious about this and he was trying very hard. But then she noticed Dominic's eyes darting away from hers, over her shoulder, then back, then over her shoulder again, and she realized that he was looking into the large arched window directly behind her, which had been affording him a clear reflection of the sex-charged extravaganza the entire time.

He noticed her noticing. "Ooh, boy," he said with a small laugh, "I guess I am busted. I'm not *dead*, you know."

"Okay, listen, Dominic," she said, moving in front of him, blocking his view of the window, then actually grabbing his face and pulling his gaze back toward her. "I do want to help. I need to think about this. I'll figure out the best possible selection of ladies for you. You need to trust my opinion and really, really try."

"Thank you, my darling," he said, his face now morphing into a *comedy* mask.

He seemed to be very close to shedding tears of joy. But as much as Cynthia loved him, she didn't trust him. His charm was a weapon that women were rarely able to defend against. She wasn't in danger of literally being wooed by him, but she knew she could be conned by him and she felt the need to call him on it.

"Dom. You are charming. Everyone knows that. But if you want to get this to work, you have to hang your charm on the wall, like a gunslinger hanging up his pistol and holster. If any woman is going to trust you, you have to give her *some small reason*."

"Okay," said Dominic, rising to his feet. "You let me know. I need to get back to work. It looks like it's starting to get crowded."

It was a little more crowded, but she couldn't help wondering what he really wanted to get back to. He walked her back to the front entrance.

"Goodbye, my darling," he said, kissing her cheek one more time. "If only *you* were looking for someone, but you still have your Max, right?"

Cynthia didn't want to even go into this with him. Even though her thing with Max was on-again-off-again at best, she had used the Max excuse several times with Dominic, when he'd come on to her in the past. It was better to let him think that. He was a friend, but not really a confidant. And although she had never been that smart about men, and even though she had always had a little crush on Dom, she had never even *considered* stepping through the doors of his revolving tiramisu case. As delicious as it sounded, that would have to be the stupidest thing a girl could ever do.

"That's right," she said, exiting toward the valet stand, "I'm off the market."

Day 1, Chapter 6

A few minutes later, while curving along Sunset Boulevard, she tried to catch up on her voicemails. Many of them were from clients. She was excited about the newcomers——she was proud of the match-ups she'd put together——and she needed to get back home to finish up the arrangements for this Friday and Saturday . . . very big date nights. One of the things that she really liked about the matchmaking business was always being up on what was going on around town. She enjoyed sifting through the social calendar and cultural listings and sending prospective couples off to expertly orchestrated evenings of burgeoning romance.

Beep. "Hi, Cynthia! Merriweather."

Merriweather was an agent at C.A.A. She was divorced, with two grown kids. She worked long hours and did not have time to go looking for men. Second Acts was perfect for this kind of successful businesswoman. Cynthia derived lots of pleasure from helping her.

Merriweather continued: "There's a little wrinkle in my Saturday. I can't wait to meet Daryl. He looks so fabulous in his running shorts. I can't believe he has actually run eleven marathons. Anyway, my daughter needs to drop her kid off at my place on Saturday . . . sort of an emergency. I might need to reschedule."

Cynthia shook her head. *Don't these people realize how hard it is to get tickets and reservations?*

She hit the *Call Back* button. Voicemail.

"Merriweather! It's Cynthia. No worries. I will find you a babysitter if I have to do it myself. I'm great with kids. How old is it? I mean, he or she. Can he . . . they . . . work a cell phone? Just kidding. I'm on it."

Another *beep*. "Cynthia, Roger here. I got your itinerary for Friday. I'm good with everything except the restaurant. I think I forgot to mention that I'm allergic to lobster. Deathly. So, I don't really think I should take Selma to a restaurant called *The Lobster*. I realize it's a romantic spot, chosen for its sweeping ocean views, but unless Selma has a thing for puffy, pimply idiots watering and wheezing through dinner and then possibly dropping dead in the parking lot, we'd better rethink. Thanks, let me know."

People. How am I supposed to know these things if you don't tell me?!

She'd change that reservation as soon as she got back. She listened to a few more voice mails as she turned onto Franklin, then finally headed up Beachwood Canyon, almost home. No major problems or hassles. The weekend roster had shaped up just fine. Better than fine. She was proud of this group. She had the strong inkling that several of these couples would really work out. Why was something so comparatively easy for them so difficult for her?

She pulled into her driveway and headed up the long, winding stairway to her front door. Her building was a three-unit art deco apartment house from 1936. She had lived on the second floor for three years. It was gorgeous and immaculate. The deco details, the view--everything. She had always been a huge fan of old movies and the feel of this place was just right.

And just recently, she had signed a lease on an incredible office space down the hill on Franklin Street, right in the neighborhood. She would move in next week. Walking distance. A rare privilege in L.A., or anywhere really. This was her neighborhood, her home base. The building housed a famous film actress-producer and a fantastic coffee house on the street level. Second Acts was on the top floor——great views, balmy breezes. She had decided it made sense to have a place clients could visit . . . a beautiful, cozy environment where they'd feel comfortable enough to open up and get personal about their wants and needs when it came to finding a mate. It would almost be like a therapist's office . . . peaceful, luxurious and perfect for her uniquely personalized service. She would have everything she needed to help clients put their best feet and faces forward: a photo and recording studio for creating professional headshots, reels, and interviews; a private workroom for writing bios; a kitchen and conference/dining room. A cappuccino machine.

It was already her neighborhood. She loved the shops and proprietors and had structured arrangements and trades with some of them for discounts and freebies for her clients. One of her favorites was The Casbah, an exclusive spa nearby where her people could go ahead of time for exotic baths (from mud to mineral to god knows what), every method of massage (from deep relaxation to something called the "The Hurts-so-good Deep-Tissue Pummeling of Punishment," which Cynthia had tried once and then couldn't get out of bed for a week . . . but she was okay with that,) to wraps (from seaweed to beeswax to an herb and oyster-infused pseudo-mummification process for men and women that involved the wrapping of all appendages, that's *all* appendages, not to mention nooks and crannies, which supposedly multiplied libido at a startling rate.) Cynthia hadn't talked to anyone who had indulged in that particular process, but then who would know, since the proprietor, Adriana Gomez, a breathtaking beauty from south of the border, signed and notarized a solemn pledge of confidentiality for all her clients. And, really, who knows what anyone's cock or breasts or balls or labia are wrapped in under one's clothes, anyway. In any case, it seemed like a good trade off for Cynthia, because if meeting and connecting with new people requires the letting go of one's defenses and being generally receptive in the erogenous zones, a trip to the Casbah was just what Dr. Feelgood ordered. If what Adriana said, that she stopped short of actual prostitution——and Cynthia did believe her, at least she was pretty sure she did——it was at least pretty much guaranteed that when clients stumbled out of there, they were more than ready for it. Any way you cut it, Adriana was at minimum a happy purveyor of high-class foreplay at five hundred dollars an hour. The Casbah and Second Acts were destined to share some clientele.

There was also a fantastic café next door that Cynthia planned to use for business or social meetings. It was owned and operated by Donald Griffin O'Brien, a charming Irish immigrant widower, who was already a good friend. Cynthia had consumed her weight in his espressos and pastries since she'd moved in up the hill four years ago. Donald got into the coffee trade by accident. He had no intention of opening a café. The Irish were not exactly known for their cappuccinos and croissants. He'd wanted to open a pub, but couldn't get a liquor license right away. So he made due with less potent fare, found success, and never made the switch. The café was really quite pub-like, though, with music and singing and darts, and a long, wooden bar that had supposedly come from the lounge of the original *Derby*, the famous, long-gone hat-shaped Hollywood haunt. And he was much more bartender than barista. He was a singer as well and seemed to know the lyrics of every rebel song, from *Kevin Barry* to *The Risin' of the Moon*, militant freedom songs that were now somewhat less in demand since the truces were signed and the troubles of the modern era had effectively ended. He constantly cursed the peace accord, since this "feckin' peacetime has feckin' decimated my singing career." By "singing career" he just meant singing in his place and that nobody wanted to hear his beloved ballads of rebellion anymore. He was ridiculously well-read and hilarious and held court like some kind of caffeine-slinging James Joyce. Meanwhile, regular customers were well aware that Donald's secret stash of hundred-year-old Irish whisky was available for the surreptitious spiking of all liquids——and solids for that matter——on the menu.

Donald was an incredible flirt and Cynthia had the sneaking suspicion that he was in love with her, but he may have just been in love with life and all its inhabitants. But he was dark too, burdened somewhat by the romantic gloom that the Irish often carry with them and he hadn't been on an actual date in the five years since his wife Katie died. Cynthia repeatedly promised him since day one of Second Acts that she'd pluck a lassie out of the bloomin' heather for him for no charge. He had been reluctant, but now, lo and behold, he finally agreed and was due to go on a date with one Adriana Gomez, that's right, the Latin queen of high-end kinky massage from three doors down. It was such a great neighborhood.

Cynthia was building a screening room to view videos and slides with clients . . . very personal, very hands-on, exclusive and pricey. So far, the business had been about applying online first and meeting her clients on the fly——in coffee shops and in their homes, but it was not the right first experience. The website would still be the first touch with her clients, but as modern as that was, Cynthia decided that what set her service apart was the personal touch. These were her people. She needed to talk to them face to face whenever possible, in a place that made them feel special. Her clients were successful, busy people and often unable to get away, so some driving would still be involved. But she was busy too and there was a limit to how much driving one person could do . . . even in L.A. *Especially* in L.A. Almost best of all, there was parking behind the building with a private entrance for discreet comings and goings . . . perfectly safe and inviting for the shy and/or camera-shy. It all might have been a tad extravagant——especially in this economy——but she was of the firm belief that planning for success was the best way to make it materialize. Plus, with the ever-growing roster of clients, she realized that she needed to hire an assistant and she really didn't want he or she wandering around her private space, rooting through her underwear drawers or whatever. She couldn't wait to get into her very own office. She had just talked to the contractor and it was almost ready. Just a few finishing touches.

She had put an ad on Craigslist and Monster and a few other places and had gotten an enormous response: one hundred and twenty–seven resumes in three days. She would read through them tonight and hopefully hire someone immediately. She needed someone smart, but also pleasant to be around. In other words, someone who wouldn't drive her bat-shit crazy. Not a lot to ask.

Speaking of which, Lolita had broached the subject of getting more involved in Second Acts sand had actually suggested she would even do it on a volunteer basis, not every week, but once in a while, when she was available. For Cynthia, just considering the logistics of Lolita's less-than-predictable commitment was almost too much to discuss. Just *thinking* about working with Lolita drove her crazy. She knew that this was another sore spot with her friend. They hadn't known each other very long, but their relationship had become a close, sisterly one——with all the good and bad connotations that implies. She had truly grown to love her, and god knows she appreciated her help in building the business. Lolita was a successful entrepreneur herself and Cynthia sought and respected her advice. But she also knew that Lolita was already busy enough. Lolita's promotional skills were the best gift Cynthia could have hoped for. More would feel unfair to both of them. Cynthia needed help from an hourly wage earner . . . not a partner.

Cynthia entered her living room, threw down her purse and briefcase, and flopped facedown onto the couch. She only realized at the moment she hit the cushion just how tired she was. It was already 4:30——a long day of driving and hanging out with ridiculously handsome men who wanted her, or at least *said* they did. Not to mention drinking bourbon, albeit with coffee, on a Thursday morning. Fun, decadent, and extremely exhausting.

Maybe she'd just get out of her business-y clothes. They weren't so business-y, this was L.A. after all, but they weren't as comfortable as the old blue sweatshirt hanging on her closet door, that's for sure. She walked to her bedroom and pulled off her high heels, skirt, blouse, and bra, and slipped the sweatshirt over her head. It was long, almost like a short dress, but not quite. So comfortable, so easy, so right. Felt like home. On any given day——it didn't matter so much what time it was, as long as she knew she had no reason to go out again——a sweatshirt was her official at-home uniform. A pair of loose white socks completed the ensemble. She had never liked slippers. They seemed too much like actual shoes, so what was the point? She liked to be barefoot in the summer, but now, in February, she liked socks. She could zip and slip around the hardwood floors. There was a little bit of *Risky Business* in the concept and although she had long outgrown her crush on Tom Cruise from that era——for a variety of reasons, obviously (not simply the Oprah couch jumping, Matt Lauer berating, his overall disturbing level of pomposity and hyperactive fanaticism, and of course "Rock of Ages," although any of these were more than enough)——she did still have a crush on him in that movie and the residual effect was that she loved being home in her underwear, wearing a soft, baggy shirt, and socks. So there.

She remembered that she needed to call Lolita. She felt pretty guilty that she'd let her misinterpret what was happening with Jack Stone, but she also really, really, *really* did not want to set her up with him. She knew it would end disastrously. It would be a mistake on so many levels: for Lolita, for Jack, and for Second Acts. Come to think of it, maybe she'd call her *later*.

She thought about Jack and laughed out loud, directly into the cushion, about how she had actually turned him down. She had never been accused of being a cock tease before, and certainly not with one of the world's biggest movie stars and possibly one of the world's biggest cocks, but she realized that it was possible that he could have interpreted it that way. She hadn't meant to lead him on.

It was the bourbon. Well, it was also him. People like him simply shouldn't be allowed to walk around being people like him and expect people like me to not even react, for god's sake.

She laughed into the cushion again.

But even though he and his legendary equipment were ready, beyond ready, hell——locked and loaded——next to the pool, he'd been so gracious when I didn't take him up on it. And so sexy.

She still wondered if she had made a huge mistake turning

him down. But, then again, what *about* Pete Blatt, the unknown quantity that Cynthia had used as a red herring to rationalize turning down Mr. Perfect? She appreciated Pete for that alone . . . for pulling her back from the brink of personal and professional disaster. But she was also oddly, almost inexplicably intrigued by the idea of seeing Pete again. There was something about that time, that place in her life——like anyone's life, she assumed——that held secrets necessary for understanding what had happened since. Maybe Pete was a clue. An incredibly cute clue. If time had served him well.

Okay, this is what Facebook was invented for.

She rolled over, swinging her feet around and planting them on the floor. She took out her laptop and turned it on, the C chord of the Macintosh start-up ringing out like a clarion call to action. Pete Blatt!

Facebook sign in: 1002 friends. Not bad. And the Second Acts page was growing even faster: 1423. She'd given away a prize for the one-thousandth "like"——a month's subscription——and that had led to a huge spurt, more than four hundred new members in three weeks. She didn't spend a lot of time working on it, but at this point there were lots and lots of satisfied customers who were hyping it better than she ever could.

Let's see, Peter Blatt. Three of them.

Pete Blatt #1: lives in Florida. Friends: 6.

She peered at the fuzzy photo. The man was sitting on a really crummy couch, wearing a white t-shirt with something spilled on the front. He was smiling. And missing one tooth. Either that or it was a dead tooth that was too dark to be seen in this horrible photograph. In a funny way, it could have been Pete. In the worst possible way--if life had really, really not treated him well. The coloring was kind of right, so that was pretty scary. She squinted at it and clicked on it to enlarge it.

Gahh! Please, oh, please, do not tell me my Pete grew up to be that.

Pete Blatt #2: lives in *California*. Okay, now we're talking. Friends: 7. Hoo boy. She screamed out loud when she saw the photo. This one was even worse. He too had the same basic coloring, but this one was clearly crystal-meth Pete. He was missing *more* than one tooth. In fact, she wasn't sure he had *any* teeth. Job: Hate. Kill. Die. Religion: Hate. Kill. Die. Favorite quote: Hate. Kill. Die.

"AHHHHHHHHHHHH!" Cynthia jumped up and ran around the room screaming. Then she burst into laughter again. She was almost positive this wasn't her Pete, but who knows? There'd been oceans of water under the bridge and maybe the bridge had fallen on top of Pete. Maybe he fell into the water. Maybe a speedboat came by and ran him over. Stranger things have happened. He was living in California, after all. But then she looked closer and he lived in Fresno. Okay, that seemed impossible.

Okay, take a deep breath. Pete Blatt #3:Lives in New York City. She was pretty sure Pete had been in the Midwest, but that was so long ago. Friends: 4,997. Whoa.

The profile picture was a dog. An actual dog. A handsome dog, but still. Okay, this Pete had a retriever. She liked this Pete better already. Interests: music. Job: music. About me: music, music, and more music. Photos: only a few. The aforementioned retriever. A picture of a guitar. Another guitar. Six, seven, eight more guitars. A picture of Bob Dylan? And some band members with some fans in the background.

Okay, this particular Pete Blatt is apparently a big Bob Dylan fan.

She scanned the fans' faces looking for clues. She closed her eyes and tried to picture his face the way she remembered it and then opened it again, hoping to catch a glimpse of it in one of these faces. She scoured all their features, looking for her Pete's nose, the one surrounded by freckles all those years ago. And then she gave up. He wasn't there. No matter how much she tried, none of those faces bore any resemblance.

She leaned back, disappointed, and took a deep breath. She closed her eyes and rubbed them with her open hands. She was tired. She removed her hands from her face and looked right into the eyes of Pete Blatt. *Her* Pete Blatt. He wasn't one of the fans, he was the guy holding the guitar, right next to Bob. Now that she recognized him, she realized he looked the same. Exactly the same. Only better. Not that he didn't look his age——although next to Dylan he seemed like a kid--I mean, who doesn't——but time had actually made him handsomer, fuller, sexier. She couldn't tell if he actually still had freckles, but he did still have the kind of a face that seemed like it should have freckles.

Send friend request? You know it. Click. *Okay.*

Now. Back to voicemails.

Cynthia leaned back on the couch and looked at the list. Her mom had called earlier in the morning, before the Pete Blatt message——it must have been just after she'd left her.

It is sometimes easier to just not listen to every message. Less aggravating. But okay, here we go.

She listened to her mother talking about how she had picked out someone from the website who she wanted to meet.

Okay . . . okay . . . okay, Mom. I need a name. What's his user I.D.? Why leave a message and not give me the number? What am I, clairvoyant, Mom? This just requires another phone call . . . another message.

She called her mother back and when she didn't pick up, she left a very short message: "Mom. User number. Please." *Click.*

She scrolled down through the voicemails. There were ten or fifteen new ones: Lolita, Lolita, Mom, Mom, Walter (Cynthia's recent ex-short-term fling who she was currently looking to match with someone to get him completely out of her life. A nice guy for someone, but not her), Merriweather (what now?), Lolita, Unknown Caller.

Wait, this Unknown Caller person has a certain appeal. Unlike a lot of these people, I don't know exactly what Mr. or Ms. Unknown Caller has to say. Beep.

"Hi, Cynthia, this is Tanya. You know, Lolita's assistant from the grooming shop? Hi, well, I heard from her that you might be looking for some help with the dating service. I love what you're doing and I'd really like to be a part of it. I've decided to leave the shop. I'm a bit burned out on dogs. I mean, I love them, but I think in the long run I might be more of a people person. Please give me a call at 323 . . ."

Cynthia smiled. She liked Tanya. She thought she was adorable. And she'd had short, but great, conversations with her over the past few months when she'd stopped by to pick up Lolita for lunch or something. She'd found out that Tanya had gone to Brown as an English major and was working on a novel. She liked the idea of hiring someone with more going on than just work. If there was one thing she knew about the matchmaking game it was that knowing things, having interests, and having a curious mind was a huge part of it. She also had gotten the strong impression that Tanya was on the same wavelength when it came to Lolita's craziness. She loved Lolita, but also knew what a piece of work she was. Cynthia was not surprised that she'd want to get out of that shop. On the other hand, she could totally imagine working with Tanya. She looked at the long list of emails with resumes attached. She looked at the clock. She was already tired and the thought of weeding through all that was about as appealing as a sharp stick in the caboose. This was a simple answer. Cynthia loved simple. This girl was a known quantity and quality. Cynthia would clear it with Lolita before making any decisions, but it couldn't hurt to just talk to Tanya.

She pressed the "Call Back" button.

Ringing, ringing . . .

"Cynthia?" asked Tanya.

"Exactly. How are you, Tanya?"

"I'm great. I'm guessing you got my message."

"Good guess. So, I'm intrigued. I think this could work.

Are you available immediately? Have you already given notice to Lolita?

"Actually, today was my last day . . . so, you know, that part's cool. I could start anytime."

"That's fantastic. Aside from the fact that I really like you, this would mean that I don't need to read more than a hundred cover letters and resumes. I think this could work out, but I'll need to get back to you tomorrow. I'm in the middle of moving my office out of the house, right down the hill into an amazing building. You'll love it. But, again, I'll call you." Cynthia would call Lolita to make sure she was fine with this. Why wouldn't she be?

"Wow, that is so cool. I'm just down the hill in Hollywood. Amazing. I really hope it works out. I look forward to hearing from you. I have a resume and I'll drop it off at your house."

Cynthia had another call coming in. Oh. My. God. It was Max. Max was back. He was overdue. He always came back. He never could stay away. Like that damn cat in that damn song. It had been four months since she had left him stark naked atop that cold, windy bluff at Zuma Beach in Malibu. She was actually pretty shocked that he hadn't called sooner. But she hadn't pined for him like she had in the past. Max contact was a nice surprise, partly because she hadn't been thinking about him. She hadn't really missed him very much.

But now that she saw his name, she did want to talk to him. If for no other reason than to hear his voice, which she would always love. A part of her hoped he was halfway around the world so that she could just have a nice conversation, say goodbye, and have it be over until next time.

"Oh, wow," said Cynthia, "you know what, Tanya? I have another call. Sure, sure, drop off the resume any time. I'll text you the address. Talk to you later."

Tanya said goodbye, buoyed with new optimism . . . confident she had a job. If this worked out it would be so amazing . . . she'd only been unemployed for a matter of hours.

Beep.

"Max."

"Sin." He always called her Sin.

"So, in what far corner of the globe might you be?"

"I'm sitting on the beach in Nadi."

"What the heck is a Nadi?"

"Fiji, baby, Fiji. Get on a plane right now and get down here. I guarantee you will never leave."

Cynthia was getting another call. Holy cow: Jack Stone.

"Um, Max?"

"Yes, Sin?"

"I'm really sorry, but I've got a business call."

"Business? What business? You mean your studio job?"

"Studio job? Are you kidding me?" This was just like Max to not remember any of the important details of her life. "Okay, Max, gotta go."

"Hey! We haven't talked in months. Who's on the phone? Who's so important?"

"It's Jack Stone."

"What, you mean *the* Jack Stone?"

"No, I'm talking about Jack Stone the plumber. Of course it's *the* Jack Stone. Gotta go."

"Wait. Sin! You would not believe the color of the ocean down here. It makes Malibu look like a black and white movie. Okay, I'll buy you a ticket. First class. How's that? Sin?"

Click. Cynthia let out a giggle. *Okay, now that was fun.*

She had set her phone to not go to voicemail until the eighth ring. She got a high volume of calls now and she often found herself in a situation where she had to take an incoming, but also needed a few seconds to wrap up with the outgoing.

Jack Stone. What on Earth is he calling about? I told him I'd get in touch when I got his list of dates together. Patience, man! C'mon, you gotta give me a little time. Not everyone on the roster is, you know, appropriate.

She took a deep breath.

"Hello, Jack?"

"Hi, Cynthia. How has the rest of your day gone?"

"Umm, well, pretty good I guess. Can't complain. How about you?"

"Actually, the rest of my day has been a little bit of a pain in the ass. I don't have an assistant anymore. Turns out Mariana did a lot more than I thought. I mean, I knew she was good, but she was some kind of organizational genius. She's been gone for half a day and my life is a total mess all of a sudden."

"Oh, well, sorry to hear that. Is that why you called?"

"Yeah, well, I was wondering if you have anyone you'd recommend? I think I might hire someone who's a little older, maybe a little less *unstable*, you know, not so prone to fantasies or whatever. This is weird to say. I hate thinking this way, but maybe someone who is a little less . . ."

"Attractive?" asked Cynthia. "Less of a temptation for you and her? Is that what you're talking about?"

"Yeah," he said, "I guess that's it."

"It's funny," she said, "I just interviewed a potential assistant myself. But she wasn't right for you. Way too cute."

"Yeah," he said. "God, I hate that."

"Yeah," she said, smiling, nearly laughing, "attractiveness sucks."

"Yeah, well, anyway . . ." he said, sounding like he was wrapping up, " . . . the other thing is, I feel kind of silly asking."

"What, you want to borrow money from me?" she asked.

Jack Stone laughed very hard and that made Cynthia laugh too. She tipped sideways onto the couch, pulling her legs up and into a fetal position, her bare knees against her bare everything else, inside the oversized sweatshirt. She loved talking and giggling on the phone; she always had. She remembered when she was a pre-teen, before everyone had their own personal communication center at their fingertips and people in households had to actually share one phone line, she would dominate it for hours at a time. She'd lie on her side in her bed, knees pulled up just like now, wrapped in a cocoon of intimacy with an entire rolodex of contacts she had developed on her own, beyond her parents' walls. It was her first memory of individuality, of grown-up self-indulgence——the first in a long string of firsts. Like all the sexual firsts, obviously, but also simple things like eating breakfast out, ordering what you want instead of what your parental units decide you'll have. Or the first time you go for two or three days with *no* contact whatsoever with your mother, for instance. My god, had that felt good. Talking on the phone was like that. She remembered feeling free and powerful, like her contact with other people in the outside world was a much-needed escape and that her mother and father could wait.

"No," said Jack Stone, after their laughter subsided, "I've got enough scratch to stretch 'til payday, thanks."

Cynthia loved how he played along with nonsense. There were a lot of men out there who weren't really that interested or willing to take a silly idea and run with it. She loved days that unfolded spontaneously and she had the distinct impression that Jack would be a real adventurer in that way, the way that Max had been too. But she was really kind of sick of Max. It was easy to imagine forgetting all other men everywhere while spending time with Jack. She felt more ridiculous than ever that she had turned him down this morning.

"Well," she said, "if you do run low, you know who to call. We could start a lemonade stand or something."

"Thanks, Cynthia," he said. "But I did have another question for you. Sort of an ulterior motive, I guess."

"Hit me," she said.

"I have tickets for this fundraiser thing tomorrow night. It's some benefit, I don't even know what for. It wouldn't be a date, I know you're seeing someone, but he shouldn't mind. It's totally platonic--kind of a client-relations thing for you. And nice company for me. You might even make some helpful connections. It's over in the Palisades at the Steve Sternberg compound."

"I know you mean *the* Steven Sternberg," she said.

"Yeah, he's a friend. Sorry. I know it's late notice. Mariana was going with me as sort of a perk for her. I said yes to that before she went all bonkers on me. Anyway, now I've got this extra ticket. I actually hate these things, with all those Depps and J-Los and Clooneys running around. Steve and his wife are cool, though."

"Are you kidding me?" she asked, sounding completely stunned.

"No, no," he said, "they'll all be there."

"No," she laughed, "I mean people actually call him *Steve?*"

Jack Stone cracked up. "People? No. I do. Actually, I usually call him the *Stever*, as in *Leave it to Stever*, but whatever. I won't even tell you what he calls *me*. It's definitely not something you'd want catching on. So, what do you think-- wanna come?"

"Does he call you Jacky? Because I was wondering if anyone did."

"No one who lived to tell the tale," he said.

"Okay, Jacky," she replied.

He laughed again. She loved messing with him and he

seemed to like it.

"I may let you live," he said, "if you come tomorrow night."

A threat. A pretty sweet threat, though.

Cynthia had seen her share of Hollywood hoopla over the years, but partying at the Sternberg palace was not one of them. She wasn't even a huge fan of his movies. She was almost always disappointed in them. But that wasn't the point. It was Leave-it-to-Stever Sternberg, for god's sake.

"Tomorrow night?" she asked, knowing full well that was what he had said. Twice. "Let me look at the calendar . . ." She wasn't actually looking at a calendar. She had rolled over onto her back and was stretching her legs toward the ceiling. She knew that tomorrow night was free. Actually not technically free. She had planned on working, just like pretty much every other night since she had launched Second Acts. "Well, I guess I could cancel the White House bash. The leader of the free world will be heartbroken, but sure, yes. Let's do it. Should I bring anything? Is it a potluck? My mom makes a mean Pepsi salad. I could probably get the recipe."

"No, that's okay. It says here Mario Batali is catering, so he probably has it covered. We could pass that recipe on to him, though. I'm sure it's hard to find a really *good* Pepsi Salad recipe. Beyonce sang a couple of songs at the last one. No telling who will show up. Listen, I can come by and pick you up? You're up in Beachwood? Let's see . . . on Verbena, right?"

She tipped over and up into a posture-perfect sitting position . . . eyes wide. Wait. Jack Stone coming to her house?

"Hold on, you don't need to do that. That's silly. It's in the totally wrong direction. Bel Air to the eastern end of the Hollywood Hills and way back over to the Palisades? That's not gallant, that's just goofus."

"Ha, ha. Goofus and Gallant--Highlights Magazine. Hilarious. No, I know, but I'll be coming from the Warner Bros. lot in Burbank. I'm meeting with Clint. I should be out of there by 3:30 or 4:00 and I can just swing over Barham and pick you up. I don't mind at all. No problem."

"Eastwood?"

"Oh, yeah, I'm sorry. Clint has this script about John Gilbert. The silent film star."

"Huge heart throb, Garbo's boyfriend. Garbo left him standing on the altar. Didn't transition into talkies. Died drunk and penniless. That John Gilbert? Now there's one uplifting bio-pic."

"Tell me about it. I love Clint and I know it would be good. But after The Artist——that silent film that's basically based on Gilbert, and of course Singin' in the Rain, arguably the greatest musical of all time, which tells the same story——the difficulty of some silent stars to make the jump to sound——I just don't know if the public would be up for yet *another* version that basically *ends* at the death and despair scene instead of overcoming it and getting all happy-dancy."

"Exactly," said Cynthia. She loved talking with him. "I mean, I'm into old Hollywood and everything, and even I wonder about it. Perhaps not a winner at the multiplex?"

"I'm not sure it's even a winner in the art house. But who knows? Clint is Clint. If anyone could pull it off. Listen, I just realized I've gotta go. I'm supposed to be Skyping with Scorcese."

Good god, what a namedropper. But is it really namedropping when every single one of your friends has a droppable name? You'd have to stop talking.

"*Skyping with Scorcese,*" she said. "Good movie title. Or a TV series? Band name? Something."

"Okay, Cynthia, see you tomorrow," he said, turning to his laptop, but forgetting to actually hang up. "Marty! How are you! Wow, *where* are you? Is that the Taj Mahal?"

"Yeah, scouting. It's beautiful. I got here fifteen minutes ago——after a nineteen-hour flight——and I already miss New York."

Cynthia realized that she was basically listening in on the first episode of Skyping with Scorcese. Should she hang up out of courtesy or just keep quiet? Maybe take notes and pitch it herself?

"Imagine how I feel," said Jack, "I miss New York every day of my life. Hold on, Marty . . . what the heck. Cynthia are you there?"

She immediately hung up. She really didn't want to try to explain that she wasn't eavesdropping. Especially because she totally *was*. She looked around the room. What a mess. Her dining room table and just about every other surface in her house was covered with files, photos, back issues of food magazines, newspapers, menus, tourism guidebooks, film schedules, museum brochures, Los Angeles-based novels and DVDs with bookmarks and post-its on *everything*. She did most of her research and planning online, but still she somehow accumulated all this *stuff*. *Everywhere*. Another reason why she needed an office.

Holy hoarder, Batman! Jack Stone is coming over.

She was usually relatively neat, but lately she'd been working really hard and eating out of Tupperware containers and leaving a garment or two . . . or three . . . oh, god . . . on the floor. Plus her cleaning lady was pregnant——about to pop, really——and she hadn't found a replacement, like she said she would. Cynthia needed to get going. She had to do a total number on the house. This was such a crazy time to go hobnobbing with Stevie and Jacky. But, come *on*.

She still had two or three details to finalize. Putting these nights together was a little bit math and science——delineating the lives and interests of two strangers, seeing where their personas intersect, and capitalizing on that intersection——and a little bit magic. She needed time to meditate on these particular people and consider them in relation to the endless permutations on the Los Angeles experience. Sort of *feel* how these people, places, and things might best fit together.

Bzzzzz. Lolita.

Day 1, Chapter 7

"C'mon, Cynthia! Pick up the phone." Lolita had tried to reach her friend several times today already and she knew she was screening. "C'mon, you little starf*cker, you." This was of course ironic, because the moniker was much more apt for *her*, and she knew it. Cynthia had never really dated anyone famous until today, at least that's what Lolita *thought*. She had no idea that Cynthia had turned him down. Knowing that would possibly cause Lolita's head to explode. On the other hand, she also didn't know that they were going out the next night on what at least *looked* an awful lot like a date.

Cynthia stared at the buzzing phone.

I have to talk to her sooner or later.

She clicked on. "Lolita, my dear!"

"Don't you dare 'my dear' me. What the hell is going on with you. I've left you at least ten messages!"

Not true. I counted them. Only nine.

"Oh really? I'm sorry. I just haven't had time to check my messages. I've been driving and talking on the phone all day. What's up?"

"What's up? If you don't fill me in on the Jack Stone operation right now, I'm coming over there and beating it out of you." She was obviously kidding, but just barely.

"Listen, Lo, nothing is going on between us. He came to me to set him up with some women . . . that's all. I'll put you onto the pile. She would do this even though she was almost sure he wouldn't be interested. But she didn't see the point of telling her the truth, saying, *Lolita, forget it. I've gotten to know him a little bit and the one thing he does not want is a woman who likes him for his E and Access Hollywood quotient.* That was the truth, but what was the point?

"So, you'll recommend me then?" asked Lolita.

"Yes, I promise.

"Because Wilfredo says we'd be good together," said Lolita.

Cynthia paused a second.

"You're talking about Wilfredo, the *Chihuahua*, right?"

"Right, he heard it from Jack's dog."

This may have been a mistake. Cynthia was appreciative of Lolita's dogs' uncanny ability to dig up new clients, but she was still skeptical when it came to Lolita's reports of these deep doggy discussions.

"Listen, Lo. I'm sure Wilfredo and Scarlett talked it over, but I wouldn't get my heart set on anything happening. Jack seems to be looking for someone more . . ." *Oh, shit. Why am I going there?*

"More what?" squeaked Lolita. "What are you talking about?"

"I don't know. I just got a vibe that what he had in mind was someone more . . ."

"More like *you?*" Lolita was steaming. She was responsible for hooking Stone into Second Acts. Well, her dogs were anyway.

"No!" squeaked Cynthia back. "God, you are paranoid."

This was something that Lolita was particularly sensitive about. She knew a little something about it. Her mother had really *been* paranoid and she hated it when people threw that term around lightly. Lolita Albion's privileged childhood had evaporated before her eleven-year-old eyes when her father took a one-way trip to Soledad Prison for pulling a gigantic Ponzi scheme. Not Bernie Madoff level, merely hundreds of millions of dollars, but decades before Madoff, so in that sense he was a Ponzi pioneer before his time. Her mother, already hanging by a thread from living in suspicion of him for years (sometimes people have reason to be paranoid) had a full-blown nervous breakdown, consumed by the demons of her unlucky chemistry, but no doubt exacerbated by her father's betrayal of trust. She died a few years later, technically from heart *failure*, but Lolita believed it to be more like a *broken* heart.

Lolita was sent to live with her father's vile sister, a bitter, lonely woman who took so little interest in her young niece, she barely noticed if she was fed and clothed, let alone nurtured. For Lolita, her real family would be her best friends, her protectors, her three furry angels: King, Max, and Wilfredo. They were always there for her. And all these many years later, defying logic, science, and mortality itself, they were still with her, still guarding over her, still there. Plus, sometimes she actually did feel paranoid and hated hearing it from Cynthia. But she had a sneaking suspicion she wasn't telling the truth about Stone and she went for it.

"Okay, so you promise me you are not going out with him?"

"Yes," said Cynthia. "I promise."

"And you also promise that you have *no plans* to go out with him, spend time with him, hang around with him, etc, etc?"

"What is this, the Spanish Inquisition up in here all of a sudden?"

"I knew it!"

"Knew what?! Lolita, what the heck is going on with

you? I need to meet with him again. So sue me! Now if you want me to include you in the list of possible dates for him, I'm happy to do it, but please, stop with the enhanced interrogation tactics!"

The volume of the conversation had been steadily building and that last part was a very loud yell, bringing it all to a screeching halt. Silence. Breathing. They both felt kind of stupid.

"I'm sorry," they said simultaneously. Then they stumbled over each other trying to establish that no, it was *me, not you*, who was out of line.

"But really," said Lolita, "I don't know what got into me. I had a really bad day and this was just a small part of it. Listen, I gotta go. I fired Tanya today, so I have a ton of work to do here."

"What? Really?" Cynthia couldn't believe it. This was not the way Tanya had characterized it.

"Yeah, well, I'll tell you about it later," said Lolita. "But I'd better get going. Okay. Talk soon. Bye-bye."

What was going on with all these assistants getting fired all day long?

Cynthia almost cut in to say that she had *interviewed* Tanya only minutes ago, but since they had just gotten past the whole Jack Stone thing, she really didn't want to blow everything up again. She'd talk to her about Tanya later, after things calmed down a bit.

"Okay," she said, "goodbye." Hoo boy.

Cynthia ate some leftovers. How did it get to be 11:30? She was tired, but really did have to clean up. She put some music on——a mix including Lady Gaga, Bessie Smith, Beyonce, Adele, Wanda Jackson, Mahalia Jackson, Joni Mitchell, and more. She'd been on an all-women-singers-all-the-time binge from all periods and genres. The more eclectic the better. She hated housecleaning with a vengeance, but something about the unlikely juxtaposition of country singer Loretta Lynn and Nicki Minaj made her happy, put a spring in her step. And in her mop.

Day 1, Chapter 8

In Beverly Hills, another cleanup was in progress. After firing Tanya, all the most distasteful parts of the dog grooming business were now, at least temporarily, Lolita's responsibility. And she hated it. A lot. In a weird way, she thought of herself as a bit of a Hollywood player. She wasn't an actress or director or producer, but being the front person of an upscale business that catered to that elite community gave her at least the convincing illusion that she was one of them, that they were her *peers*. Having to spend two hours at the end of the day vacuuming fur and scraping canine excrement from tabletops, when those "peers" were out sipping fine wine and doing their part to put the *lounge* into the Polo Lounge, brought the whole situation into clearer focus.

She turned to King, Max, and Wilfredo, who were watching her with concern. "You know, guys," she said, "I'm not part of the elite of this town. I'm a peon, a lackey, a grunt. This shop and my life may sometimes have a slight patina of glamour, but it's all a lie. This is a pathetic bottom-feeding enterprise!"

She looked at her hands.

"Dammit!" she cried. "Look at this. I have dog shit under my nails! No offense."

"None taken," said King. The other two dogs nodded their heads in agreement.

"And I have fur all over me!" she whined.

"So do we," all three dogs whined back.

Lolita usually appreciated their senses of humor, but not now.

"Very funny," she said. "But I also have it in my nostrils! Goddamn it. This is not my job!"

She dreaded the process of interviewing new people. She knew that she could be difficult and that in some ways, Tanya had been the perfect match--easy going, happy to do what needed to be done, and also a very attractive second banana when Lolita needed a day off or just wanted to play hooky. She knew for a fact that some of the younger clients——male *and* female——were coming in for Tanya, not for her. And not for the grooming. Tanya had really been the only employee who had ever worked out. The three before her were disasters. One actually *robbed* her. It was hard to find trustworthy, competent people and, in many ways, Tanya was a godsend.

Lolita washed her hands, locked up, and loaded the three dogs——one tiny, one large, and one enormous——into her adorable red sports car. She pulled out of the alley, and back around to Beverly Drive, slowing and stopping across the street from the shop. She stepped out onto the sidewalk and leaned on her elbows on the roof of the coupe that Dog Groomer to the Stars had provided. The dogs looked on from inside the car. God, she loved her business. She loved the neighborhood. Talk about location: Beverly Drive, between Santa Monica Boulevard and Brighton Way, two doors down from the Museum of Radio and Television, across the street from Taschen Books, tons of exclusive shops, a block from Rodeo Drive. The fact that she had even gotten in there was an absolute miracle. The landlord was a dog lover. Lolita gazed lovingly at the shop. It had been her dream and she made it come true with a combination of hard work and pure force of will. She had built something here.

"Get her back," said King.

"But how?" she asked, staring at the beautifully etched and backlit copper sign she had designed for over the door.

"Apologize," said Wilfredo in a whispery, nearly inaudible growl.

"Apologize," she repeated, turning to the three of them. "You're right."

So she would call Tanya and apologize. She had to get her back. She would give her a raise. Maybe more perks . . . like better bonuses or even a small piece of the business. Whatever it took.

She got back in the car, stuck in her ear buds, and speed-dialed her soon-to-be rehired assistant. She pulled out into traffic, happily watching the well-heeled pedestrians, feeling absolutely blessed to be there. This was her neighborhood. This was her world. As long as Tanya was responsible for cleaning it when it got dirty, all was right in that world. She turned left onto Wilshire Boulevard. Ringing . . . ringing.

"Lolita?" answered Tanya, surprised to be hearing from her.

"Yes!" she said, relieved to hear her voice. "Tanya. How are you? I mean, wow, what a day, right?"

"Uh, yeah," said Tanya, wondering where this was going. "You could say that."

"Well, first, I want to say how sorry I am about today. I mean, what you did was very inappropriate, but that's behind us now. And you were right. I've been guilty of some pretty wacky behavior myself from time to time. I see myself in you."

"You see *yourself* in me?" asked Tanya, not exactly taking it as a compliment.

"Yes, that's why I hired you. Sure I got pissed off today, but I want to tell you that there are no hard feelings on my end. Consider yourself un-fired. Let's pretend none of this even happened. So, that's it! See you in the morning?"

Long pause. Not because Tanya didn't know the gist of what she was going say. She was just trying to determine the best way to put it.

"Wow," she said. "You came dangerously close to issuing an apology there."

"No, no," said Lolita, turning onto North Canon Drive. "I definitely apologized. I used the word sorry, I remember."

"Yeah, you said you were sorry for what *I* did. Listen, Lolita. Whatever. The fact is, though, I think I already have another job."

"What? No you don't. You're kidding, right?"

"Nope. Not kidding."

"Another dog shop? I was totally going to give you a raise anyway, so I'll definitely match what they're paying you."

"Nope. Not another dog shop. Listen, Lolita. We had a good run, but I'm in the mood for a change. I'm doing something totally different."

"What is it, if you don't mind me asking."

Tanya thought it might be unwise to divulge that information at this juncture. "Doesn't matter," she said.

"Just something else."

"Tell me, Tanya!" shrieked Lolita. It seemed like every drop of blood in her body rushed directly to her head. Her pulse was pounding in there like a kettledrum.

"Listen," said Tanya, "I don't need this."

"No, wait, hold on!" cried Lolita. "Tanya! Why are you doing this to me? I'm sure we can work it out!"

Lolita knew it wasn't safe to drive under the influence of what she was feeling at that moment. She clutched the wheel like a lifeline, spied a parking space and headed for it, aiming like a drunk person playing darts, somehow thinking that through mere concentration, she could overcome her hugely debilitating impairment . . . in this case, hurt, jealousy, and rage. She veered hard to the right——all three dogs howling with alarm——and slammed into the rear of a parked car.

It happened to be a Beverly Hills Police cruiser.

The two cops inside both banged their heads on the dashboard like synchronized crash dummies. They weren't seriously hurt, but they were seriously infuriated. They inspected the damage to their car and the one in front of them, and the one in front of *that*.

They ambled toward Lolita like twin John Waynes. One leaned down to ask if she were okay, but she didn't answer because she was still talking into her phone:

"Tanya? Hello? Are you there? Can you hear me now?"

Unfortunately, Tanya couldn't hear her because she had hung up just before the crash. Also unfortunate was the fact that, when asked to see her license, after scrambling through her belongings, she realized that she'd left her purse at the shop. The officers were not amused.

It also didn't help that the dogs all growled at them with such fury that they had to radio animal control.

Lolita, accustomed to finessing difficult situations, couldn't charm her way out of this one. They took the dogs to the city pound and hauled Lolita downtown. Downtown Beverly Hills, but still. Her one phone call was to Cynthia, partly because she was a good friend who Lolita knew she could count on despite their recent difficulties, and partly because she just wanted to scream at her.

Unfortunately, though, when Cynthia's phone buzzed, she didn't hear it. She was working up some serious sweat equity with a vacuum in the living room. Moments before, Cyndi Lauper had come up on the mix, and Cynthia, closely related to her in spirit and name, had turned it way, way up.

The phone rings in the middle of the night,

My father yells "What you gonna do with your life?"

Oh, daddy, dear,
You know you're still number one,
But girls,
They wanna have fun.

Day 2, Chapter 9

Cynthia woke up at 8:15. She showered and dressed and started a pot of coffee. Trying to eat more healthfully, she grabbed a yogurt and an apple and turned on her laptop. By the time the computer had fully booted up and the coffee was ready, she had already finished eating, so, just to have something to go with the coffee and as a reward for her original dietary restraint, she grabbed an oversized square of coffee cake, leftover from a brunch she'd had with Lolita a few days earlier.

Lolita, she thought: fantastic and infuriating. Fantastically infuriating. Cynthia remembered her words——"I'm way worse than your mother"——and realized just how true that statement was. They were so different in so many ways, but they really did have some similarities: loving and loyal, but erratic and in need of attention. A lot of attention.

Approximately every waking hour of every day. How had she started yet another relationship that mirrored the one with her mother? How could this happen this far down the road of life? She supposed it was because it seemed so comfortable, even when it was *un*comfortable. And she really did love her and love being around her. Since first meeting, they had had a number of hilarious adventures together. So much fun. Being with her in public was a blast, always walking a fine line between hilarity and unmitigated social embarrassment.

Like the time about a month earlier when they went on a road trip north to Montecito for a wedding of an old college friend. It was an exclusive affair. It was at the Four Seasons Biltmore, right on the beach, a short walk from Oprah's house. Theoretically, that is. Oprah actually came in a car. Somehow, the alchemy generated by their two personalities made Cynthia and Lolita the life of the party. They did their share of dancing with a variety of single men, from baby billionaire inventors to no less than three recently divorced reality-show producers. You simply cannot predict what will happen with open access to that much incredible champagne for that many hours in one day. It started at 2:00 PM and by 9:30, Lolita was slow dancing with the best man, the creator of a very popular sitcom, and Cynthia was doing the same with the mayor of Santa Barbara, whose wife had passed out in the lounge. Cynthia and the mayor were mostly concentrating hard, trying to put into practice a few almost-recalled ballroom dance moves they'd only half-picked-up over the years. Their behavior was almost totally innocent. Almost. But then Cynthia caught a glimpse of Lolita and her partner and realized that his hands were all over her——right there in plain view of the bride, the mother of the bride, and the mother of the mother of the bride——his arms snaking around, his hands down the small of her back to her ass, then back up, the hem of her short skirt trailing with them, his fingers inching up under her red, beaded, bombshell top, under which Cynthia knew for a fact there was nothing, just her more than ample ampleness.

Cynthia cast herself off from the mayor, coming to the defense of her friend's honor, declaring, "Unhand her, sir!" After she said it, she realized it sounded less intimidating and more formal than she had intended, like old-movie speak, but it did work. The man retracted his tentacles and everything stopped for a moment. But then Lolita replied, "Cynthia, my dear, I want to thank you from the bottom of my heart for your kind assistance in dealing with this untoward interloper." Then, clutching the guy's wrist and placing his hand back on her breast, she issued a direct order to her friend: "Now, please leave us alone so that said untoward interloper can proceed with getting even more untoward." They all looked at each other and laughed hysterically. Cynthia returned to her mayor, who spun her 'round and 'round like a top, the only move he actually remembered, adding exponentially to the potency of the bubbly. Unfortunately, as had often been the case, Lolita's dancing-mauling partner failed to mention that he was in fact married and his wife, a well-known actress, delayed on a flight from Barcelona, arrived ten minutes later, just as her husband's lips, which had been exploring the nuances of Lolita's lovely neck and collarbone, plunged from that precipice down the salty slope of her right breast. It was a beautiful moment but it ended ugly. This was the story of Lolita's life in a lot of ways. She didn't go looking for trouble, exactly. She was just very, very good at finding it. But the night wasn't lost. No one died, no blood was shed——well, not too much anyway——and the two friends ended the evening by walking it off through the streets of Montecito together, singing and plotting their perfect romantic futures with honest-to-goodness true loves. Cynthia meant it. She wasn't so sure about Lolita.

In any case, she valued their friendship very much and all of Lolita's support. Even Lolita's strange dogs had pitched in. Cynthia knew that she would never stop trying to help Lolita find someone to love even though she was pretty sure that

Lolita, in spite of what she said, would never settle down. She had to call her. But Lolita was not an early morning person. It would have to be later.

Cynthia needed to check on the details of a few dates, but she looked out the window at the miraculous Los Angeles morning and suddenly had the urge to go for a walk. She wanted to think, to get a little centered . . . prepare for seeing Tanya, for Lolita, for discussing her mother's choice for a date——something she hadn't actually checked out yet—— and later, for going to the Sternberg soiree with Jack Stone. She already knew what dress she'd wear. It was cleaned and ready. The house looked better than it had in days. Now she needed to clean her head a bit too with an early-morning get-away, like a mini-vacation. A brisk loop around the canyon would do the trick. She might do her normal walk, plus maybe even go farther and gaze admiringly at the new building on Franklin for a bit.

She laced up her walking sneaks and headed out into the perfect morning. The orange tree in her front lawn was blossoming and its exquisite fragrance stopped her in her tracks. She pulled off one small flower, squeezed it between her fingers and brought it to her face, breathing it in like some kind of magic aromatherapy potion, which it sort of was. That scent was high on her list of reasons she loved living there.

She turned up the block, a steep stretch that was a daunting way to start, but she loved it. She loved having to power through the toughest part early, so that everything else seemed easier. She took her phone out of her pocket to check the time: 9:13. There were a bunch of new emails, voice mails, but she'd read them later. This was why she had her phone on silent——she needed some peace and quiet. But then she noticed something else. There were several notifications on Facebook. So and so liked this, so and so commented on that. But one got her full attention, and fast:

Pete Blatt accepted your friend request. Write on Pete's wall.

Cynthia came to a complete stop and stared at the screen. Pete. Blatt. She pictured him again in her room in the valley. She thought of his young voice and his sweetly sincere love for her and how, in retrospect, it was so devoid of cynicism. Even way back then, when he'd obviously been operating under the influence of raging teen lust, she also had the feeling that his adoration of her went way beyond that. That he worshipped her inside and out in the best possible sense.

She walked into the shade of a gnarly California Oak to get a look at his page out of the sunshine, seeking to parse more info, now that she had so-called friendship access.

Bingo: phone number. Bingo: street address. Wait a minute . . .

Cynthia literally smacked her forehead in disbelief, like a dumb guy in a movie. Pete Blatt lived at 6138 Glen Tower Street, just blocks from where she was standing at that very moment. This was insane. She'd been walking this neighborhood for years. Had she passed him? Had they not recognized each other? No, that's right. He had just moved back to L.A. recently.

She leaned against the tree for a moment, catching her breath and thinking about how incredible this was. Should she knock on his door? How crazy would that be? Pretty crazy. She decided to make a slight change in her usual walking route. She'd just pass his house, check it out, whatever. She would not go up to the door, definitely not.

She continued up the hill, twisting along, and despite the increasing steepness, she picked up the pace even more. She took a right at Cheremoya Drive and bumped into her neighbor, Celeste, an eighty-year-old retiree who had worked in animation in the fifties and sixties, first at Disney, where she painted backgrounds for *Peter Pan*, among other films. She liked to talk.

"Cynthia, my dear, how are you," she asked.

"Oh, fine, Celeste," she said, slowing down, but trying not

to actually stop, hoping Celeste would let her continue on her way.

"My, you're in a hurry this morning, honey," Celeste said. "Isn't it too perfect of a morning for that?"

"Yeah, well," said Cynthia, walking backwards up the hill now, trying to be polite, but really not wanting to get hooked into a long conversation about the old days, Celeste's specialty. Not now. "I have a lot on my schedule today, unfortunately. So, you know, great seeing you and next time we'll chat a bit more. Have nice day."

"Yeah, right. Well, so far it hasn't been all that *neighborly*. Did I ever tell you about the time that Walt came into my office and told me I was the best painter he ever had?"

"Yes, yes, you have. Great story and I'm sure he was right. You are a remarkable talent." And she was. Cynthia loved her and her work. But. Not. Today. She turned around and picked up the pace, and then looked back over her shoulder to see Celeste glaring at her, arms folded.

"Celeste, see you soon!"

She reached the next corner, North Beachwood Drive, and took another right. She couldn't recall how many blocks farther up the hill it was, and she was breathing heavily now, partly because of the terrain and partly because of the mountain of nostalgia she was climbing inside her head.

She passed Glen Green Street on the right and then, thirty seconds later, she came to Glen Tower Street on the left. This was it, complete with a dead end sign. No outlet. Was this sign some kind of *sign?* Well, maybe not, but the no outlet thing made her snooping slightly more conspicuous.

She headed down the block, passing houses, trying to locate any numbers at all. One thing about this neighborhood was that the houses ran the gamut--everything from ramshackle ticky-tacky boxes from the sixties to restored Spanish-styles and Craftsmans, nearly all occupied by industry people.

6122. 6124. 6130. Cynthia couldn't believe how much of a thrill this was. She remembered that Pete had had an obsession for riding past her house on his bicycle, and here she was, decades later, walking past his.

6132. 6134. 6136. She stopped and stood behind a short palm tree, the kind that resembles a huge pineapple, finally squinting and seeing 6138, the number she was looking for, just twenty or so yards ahead. It was the last house on the block, the very end of the dead end. Impossible to *pass*, really. The only reason one would need to be in front of it would be if it were your actual destination. Or, you know, if you were clumsily casing the joint. It was a tall Spanish-style structure, lovingly restored, and similar to hers in a way. Soft music drifted subtly from an open window. It was old-time music.

Scratchy even——like a Victrola——a lovely swinging melody and rhythm, violin and guitar intertwined. Together with the vintage house, the music evoked another era, like Cynthia had walked back in time, way past her childhood, past her mother's childhood, to 1920s or '30s Hollywood, back when this house was built.

She thought about walking up to the door. How bad could it be, really? Well, pretty bad. What if he turned out to be an awful guy? Musicians can be pretty weird. Up all hours; high . . . most of them. They lead pretty vampire-ish lifestyles. What if he had become a first-class asshole? What good would it do to *know* that? Or what if he *hated* her or barely remembered her and only accepted her friendship to be polite and had absolutely no interest in knowing her at all? That, of course, was the dark side of social networking. Well, one of the dark sides. She stared up at the window, the curtains sailing gently in the breeze. She had serious second thoughts about the whole thing. She just was not that interested in finding out something bad today.

Before this nonsense started, she was on track for having a very good day and she didn't want to spoil it. She would think about the whole Pete Blatt thing and revisit it later. At least that way she could savor the fantasy of what he might have become and what meeting him might be like——the storybook version. Yes, good decision. She looked at her phone: 9:42. She would walk back around the neighborhood, get a good, long walk in, and go home in time to meet Tanya.

She turned, pushing off hard from the sidewalk to make a speedy departure from the street of Pete, and immediately crashed into a fellow pedestrian, who, having raised his arms in an attempt to prevent the collision, squarely placed his open hands onto her breasts like he was checking the ripeness of cantaloupes.

"Oh, my, excuse me, I'm so sorry," he said, while Cynthia said something more like, "Hey! Watch it! What the hell?"

Realizing she had dropped her phone, she bent down to retrieve it. "Oh, man. I just *got* this thing. Oh, please, oh, please. Don't be broken."

That's when the man whispered, "Cynthia? Amas? Is it still Amas?"

And Cynthia, looking up and into the familiar dark eyes of her former adolescent crush, replied, "Pete? Pete Blatt? What on Earth are *you* doing here?"

She didn't really listen to what he said next, because she obviously knew the answer to that question. She was focused on the area around his nose, where——low and behold—— there still appeared to be a few freckles.

"I'm so sorry," said Pete, sounding a little deeper in pitch, perhaps, but still remarkably like he did at sixteen. "Is your phone okay? I live right over here. It's so weird that you just contacted me on dumb old Facebook and now we bump into each other. Literally."

"I know, well, yeah, it is. But I live a few blocks from here."

"You've got to be kidding me," said Pete.

"No, I walk around here all the time. I'm surprised we haven't seen each other sooner."

"Oh, well, I just moved in. Hey, how about I fix you a cup of coffee and we can make sure the phone is working. If not, I'm replacing it."

Cynthia stared at him. What he looked and sounded like and what he was saying--it all made her happy. "Yeah, sure, I'd love that," she said, as they headed side-by-side toward the house. "It is, by the way."

"It is what?"

"My name. It's still Amas. It wasn't for a short time, but I got it back."

"Glad to hear it," said Pete Blatt, opening his front door, which he had left unlocked.

Day 2, Chapter 10

Lolita hadn't spent the *whole* night in jail, but it felt like it. As incarceration goes, doing time in Beverly Hills isn't all that uncomfortable, but still, jail is jail. After failing to reach Cynthia, she tried Tanya, who also didn't pick up. She finally got her lawyer, Arthur Robbins, on the phone. He was a short, wide, furry man with a ridiculous mustache and more hair on his back than most men have on their heads. He was also the most loyal friend she had, partly because he truly lusted after her. He was like a neighbor who does favors for the lady down the block for years on the remote chance that when she passes, it will be revealed that she has bequeathed the secret millions in her mattress to him. In terms of Arthur ever receiving any carnal remittance from Lolita, he was seriously deluded. Hers was a mattress from which he'd never yield any return on his investment whatsoever. But still, he never let her pay for his services, and she had let it go on for years, clearly knowing his motives and just as clearly restating every single time that he would never, could never buy her love, no matter what the price.

He came and bailed her out.

"You know," said Arthur, opening the door of his massive black Mercedes, "we would make an excellent team."

"Arthur," she said, sliding across the leather seat, "I'd be happy to pay you with money you know."

"Don't be silly, I wouldn't think of it," he said, pulling onto Rexford Drive, heading toward her house.

He walked her to her door, where she thanked him and said goodbye. Later, in the afternoon, after she got some rest, Arthur would return and bring her to the city lot, where her mangled car had been impounded. They would have it towed to the shop. Then he would take her to the other kind of pound and pick up King, Max, and Wilfredo, poor things. Ultimately, this shouldn't have been that big of a problem, but in Lolita's current state of mind it was one gigantic pain in the ass. She blamed two friends who almost seemed to be conspiring against her: Cynthia and Tanya. But that was just crazy. They barely even knew each other, right? Lolita had no idea that Cynthia had interviewed Tanya for a job, that Cynthia was planning on asking Lolita if she would mind if she *hired* Tanya, and that, pending her blessing, they'd literally be working together.

Good god, what a night. She knew she'd fall asleep in a matter of moments. She inhaled deeply, and then released the kind of down-to-your-core inhale-exhale that almost always pries open the gates to dreamland. But before she passed through, she smelled something pretty foul that she immediately blamed on the dogs. Specifically, Wilfredo. He was much smaller than the others, but far more pungent. But then she realized that, of course, the dogs weren't even there. She lifted her pillow over her head to at least block out the morning sunlight and instantly determined that the source of the stench was none other than herself. One simply does not work all day, shovel dog poop for two hours, spend four hours in jail, and come out smelling like a rose.

She got up and took a shower, which, despite her fatigue, jolted her like a triple espresso and kicked her mind back into gear regarding Tanya, Cynthia, and everything else. She would not be falling asleep anytime soon. She called Cynthia again: nothing. She called *Tanya* again: also nothing. She *texted* Cynthia: nothing, nothing, and more nothing. She looked at the clock on the wall: 10:37 AM.

That's it. I'm going over there. I'll pick up the dogs first.

She got halfway down the front stairs before she remembered

she didn't have a car.

Dammit, Dammit, Dammit.

She was not accustomed to being stymied at every corner like this. She was Lolita, dammit.

Wait. The Vespa. But no. It's a fantastic mode of transportation, but not terribly effective for hauling four hundred and fifty pounds of dog.

She called Arthur and got his voicemail.

"Arthur, it's me. Hi, sweetie." She wasn't proud of that *sweetie*. She knew he was susceptible to her flirtation and she really, really tried hard not to resort to it. But this was an emergency. "Listen, honey, can you believe it? Something else has come up. Could you do me a huge favor and deal with the car, you know, have it towed over to Henry's Service Station. Oh, and Arthur. Also pick up the dogs?"

She felt bad about this. She would have much preferred to pick up her darlings herself. But that was impossible with the tiny scooter and, besides, Arthur was just about the most dependable creature on Earth, at least to her. At least some of that loyalty was stoked by the most potent fuel known to mankind: eternal hope against hope for potential pussy. But she didn't hold this against him . . . she really liked him very much. But not in that way. It was just the way it was.

"The extra key is still hidden you know where," she

continued. I know it's a lot to ask. You are such a friend. Thanks, honey. Kisses."

She really wasn't at all worried about Max, King, and Wilfredo, who were perfectly capable of taking care of themselves. They had taken care of her for years, after all. But she didn't realize until after she hung up just how tall of an order all that was. Arthur could handle the car thing fine, but her three dogs were not always all that cooperative, especially with a man who had been hitting on her for years, without so much as a shred of evidence that that sort of attention was desired on her part. They had never taken too kindly to him.

She had a thought and called back. Voicemail.

"Hi. Me again. Hey, I know that my sweet boys haven't always been your biggest fans. I suggest you bring beef. Kobe. Lots of it. Okay, that should do it. I'll call you later. Thanks again. Bye, honey. Sweetie. I can't tell you how much I appreciate it. Let's have dinner later this week. You are the best. Oh, and watch your wallet."

Good god.

She went to the garage and unzipped the black leather cover, revealing her immaculate pink Vespa. She hadn't used it in quite a while. It was her baby. She had ridden it up Coldwater Canyon countless times to Maximillian Schell's house, back in the day. He even started calling her clitoris her Vespa, as in, "Darling, would you mind terribly if I took your sweet little pink Vespa for a ride tonight?" It was dumb, but she loved his accent and somehow it made the scooter ride over feel turbo-charged with erotic anticipation. Zipping through that neighborhood, past those houses and those magnificent lawns——the engine purring happily beneath her——was a powerful aphrodisiac. She was living the dream, mixing with Hollywood royalty. It was her ultimate fantasy--the same one that seemed to be crumbling around her now.

Soon she was humming along Sunset Boulevard. She would talk to Cynthia, who would talk to Tanya, and all would again be right in her world.

Day 2, Chapter 11

Cynthia was well aware that her phone was filling up with every kind of attempted communiqué. But this was Pete Blatt. Time travel is a superpower not yet readily available every day of the week.

While Pete made coffee, Cynthia wandered through his living room. It was like a museum of musical instruments. Mostly strings. It was amazing to her that his childhood interest had taken hold so completely it truly seemed he was put on Earth for this one thing. The place was also lined with bookshelves filled with the most incredible collection of books she'd ever seen. The wall was covered with art. Unique stuff. Personal. Meaningful. Not dispensable. Even though he'd just moved in, it felt warm, lived in, and wall-to-wall fascinating. A racing bike hung on the far wall. Of course. The freckly kid with the perpetual hard-on had a perpetual hard-on for life.

He seemed to have every possible variation of guitar, ukulele, banjo, mandolin, lute, zither. Incredible. There were some that defied definition, at least to Cynthia.

"What's this crazy thing that looks like a harp connected to a guitar?" she asked.

Pete came around the corner with two cups and a smile. "Strangely enough, it's called a harp *guitar*," he said, rolling his eyes. "They've been around for a couple of hundred years. They were popular in the U.S. early in the twentieth century, but they're pretty much out of vogue now, except for crazy music history nuts and musicians. Or both, like me. I've always loved the way the harp part is like an arm and that the instrument almost looks like it's playing itself. It doesn't in case you're wondering."

"That's a relief," said Cynthia, sipping what may have been the most perfect cup of coffee she'd ever tasted. "Do you play it?"

"Not that often, but sure, once in a while."

"How about now?" she asked.

"Now? Okay, but you'd better watch out. I never need to be coaxed to play. You might learn to regret it."

"Try me," she said, easing onto the couch and placing her coffee on the table it's named after.

Pete eased the antique instrument from the wall and sat next to her. She wondered if he remembered how closely this mimicked that day, way back when, that they sat together in her living room. On the couch. When he'd played her guitar.

"Is it just me," she asked, toasting him with her coffee, alluding to the Pisco they'd shared, "or do you also sense a bit of déjà vu rolling in here?"

"Like a freight train," he said, toasting back. "I've thought of that afternoon often. You know, it's weird. I mean, I hesitate to mention this, but I'm not sure if you knew. I absolutely worshipped you and everything about you. That was a very big day for me. A big day that unfortunately ended very badly."

"Well, yes," she said. "But, you know, the worship was appreciated. I liked you too and I like you now. Even that bad ending has improved with age. Like wine. Or Pisco. Whatever. I think it's the screw-ups you remember *most* fondly. Maybe it's because from a distance it's funny and but also sweet. You remember the dumb things that kid did— —things you learned from——and it makes you really *love* that kid. We share a memory of two dumb kids and we both love both of them. Something like that, although it came out kind of stupid."

"No it didn't," said Pete. "It came out just right."

"Yeah, well, anyway," she said, sliding deeper into the cushion, "let's hear it. What does one play on a harp guitar?"

"Well," he said, tuning the strings quickly and precisely— —and there were a lot of them, "way back it was mostly a classical instrument in Europe, but in the U.S. people starting using them more for song-based music, in small bands. It added a nice blend: the picking and strumming of the guitar, together with the harp's heavenly aura. I have used it occasionally in a more unorthodox way. I brought it along to a session and ended up using it in a recording of that old W.C. Handy song *Hesitation Blues*. Lots of people have sung it, Louis Armstrong, Janis Joplin, Taj Mahal. It's been recorded dozens of times. I could try that."

"I'm waiting," she said, drumming her fingers lightly on the side of his guitar with mock impatience.

He paused momentarily just to look at her. He liked her playfulness. He was recalling and confirming what he loved about her face, like returning to a beautiful painting after many years. The memory had become abstracted and was now being reinvigorated by her presence.

She gazed back at him, realizing that she'd had no idea when they were young, that he really had amazing eyes, the kind that completely close during a smile and then reopen, revealing the depth of his pleasure, the sincerity in his heart.

She could feel her admiration and affection for him welling up inside, rising like a tide.

He started plucking out the melody gently on the harp. It *was* heavenly and ethereal, despite the familiar blues form. Then he switched down to the guitar and beat out the bluesy bass line, quietly, but with ringing clarity, each string delineated with crisp expressiveness. It was obvious he was a master player. She adored the music *and* the encounter. Both were simultaneously nostalgic and new. Pete was unlike anyone she'd known in her adult life. On paper he would probably sound a bit geeky . . . an old-music freak, a collector. That could sometimes evoke the stale, dustiness of antique shops and auction houses. But he was remarkably vibrant, handsome, capable, soulful, and strong. And those eyes.

She thought about the unlikely events of the last two days. Jack Stone coming on to her and she turning him down. She'd had pangs of regret. It was potentially a classic blunder. A real award winner. But she knew it was the right thing to do and was actually proud of herself for keeping her professional life intact. In the past, there were so many times she had allowed her screwed-up love life to sidetrack her work and wreak havoc. Plus this thing with Pete seemed so right. Her heart felt absolutely full. There was something about Pete she truly adored.

Then he got to the singing part and his voice was devastating too. Not particularly perfect or trained, but warm and deep and easy——part Elvis, part Sinatra, part universal lover——speaking to something deep within, something she herself was not fully aware of.

Rocks in the ocean, baby,
Fish in the sea,
They all know you mean the world to me.
Tell me how long do I have to wait?
Can I get you now or must I hesitate?

Hesitating was totally out of the question. She knew that he knew that she didn't want to wait. It might have been the longing in her eyes or the trembling of her lips, but it was probably the same thing that always, always, always gave her away. Her cheeks were glowing like a red neon invitation.

He gently slid the large stringed instrument onto the rug and moved in for a soft, sweet kiss.

"I feel like I should tell you," he said, "that I'm leaving on tour. I'm . . ."

She interrupted him with a sweet kiss of her own, whispering, "All the more reason, sweet Pete."

Sweet Pete. That spilled from her lips so easily, even though she'd totally forgotten she'd called him that. The years fell away, like they were back in her old house on her old street, when the world was new. He cupped the small of her waist and moved his hand upward, taking it slowly——seeming to feel some of the shyness he'd had when they were young. It was as if being with her brought back the tentativeness he had left behind long ago. But she loved it. She loved his sweetness. It was a side most men are afraid to show, but Pete seemed as nervous and excited as a teenager to find himself in this situation. It felt illicit and rebellious in a way that grown-up relationships never feel.

They were both wearing loose, casual clothing that, as they disrobed, seemed to instantly vanish, as if simply melting away. They sat facing each other, their bodies familiar, yet totally different: he, more defined and muscular . . . she, more voluptuous. She smiled at his erection, bending over and kissing its head, as if greeting a long, lost friend. She remembered his perpetual boner, when her mother had come home unexpectedly——him smiling cordially, trying to act naturally, his rod, 100% due-north vertical, resonating rigidly with his every move, like a flesh-and-blood Geiger counter under his gym shorts——the skimpiest of cotton, no underwear. He headed down the front steps to his bike and still, still, still was hard as he rode away, like the circus had come to town and pitched a big top in his pants. It was a funny, embarrassing thing, but so sexy and such a sweet memory. She remembered wondering if it had lasted the whole trip home like that. Now it almost felt like it had *never* gone away, like this was its natural state. She smiled slightly, thinking of it throbbing and twitching away the years, like it was gunning for her through the decades, and had finally hunted her down.

And as if Pete could read her mind, he also smiled, breathing deeply, softly whispering, "You're more beautiful than ever."

But then, without saying a word, together they chose to hold back, to not dive in hastily. They just looked at each other. This revision of the past would be slow and deliberate. They wanted to savor everything. In a swirl of drunken delirium the first time around, this weekday morning they were simply buzzed on French roast . . . just about as sober as sober gets. Slowly, silently, they touched and tasted each and every body part with the utmost sensuality, taking a highly erotic inventory. He placed his hands on her knees and then ever-so-slowly moved them toward her, along her tingling thighs, his thumbs hooking gently around and under, causing her to let out a soft sigh, her mouth opening slightly, her eyes gently closing. She mirrored his movements, *her* hands traveling the same journey down *his* thighs, her thumbs softly brushing past his balls, her fingers reaching his erection and gently, sweetly twanging it like she had so many years ago, except this time almost in slow motion, not flippantly playful, but erotically, achingly so. She smiled and opened her eyes and he was smiling too . . . remembering.

He moved toward her, leaning onto one knee and tenderly lowering her down, one hand cradling her head, the other at the small of her back, expertly coaxing her center of gravity toward him. He descended too, first kissing her knees, then her thighs.

"No tan line," he whispered.

"You remembered," she replied, gently biting her lower lip as his tongue crept deeper, approaching, then exploring her *other* lips. She inhaled sharply and eased out a shuddering exhale. His open palm glided slowly up her belly, to her right breast, first lingering, caressing the often-neglected underside, then incrementally over the top, her nipple anticipating his fingertips. He drew close and entered her slightly, stopping to tease that lovely moment, that delicious spot, hips barely moving, applying just enough pressure to torture them both a bit, hovering on the edge, massaging the soft, hard, warm wetness. Her hands gripped his flexed haunches, as she tried in vain to squeeze him closer. But he resisted, holding steady.

Holy Jesus, fuck me, she said to herself, digging her nails in, demanding more, but he refused, refused, refused, teasing and toying with her sweetest of sweet spots until she gasped loudly at a pitch that seemed to be an octave up from anything she could ever recall hitting, "Please, Pete! For Christ's sake, Pete! Fuck me, Pete! Fuck me!"

He paused, feeling lightheaded, but redeemed and unbelievably lucky to finally have the opportunity to override the old embarrassment. Realizing that although the couch had served them well so far, it was not the appropriate theater of operations for what would happen next, he pulled her close and whispered, "Hang on," his lips brushing gently the inside of her ear, and hoisted her——smoothly, effortlessly, remaining deeply implanted, united, conjoined, skewered, plugged-in, and hard-wired for maximum combustion—— transporting her to his bedroom. He stopped for a moment in the doorway——too disoriented by desire to take another step——and softly placed and firmly pinned her against a wall covered with a large, lush tapestry that looked like something from the Renaissance or the Middle Ages or from way, way back before that. It was very possibly the most beautiful work of art she had ever seen, much less splayed and screwed upon. He inched even higher inside her, up on his tiptoes, then letting her down slightly, then up again, pausing for a moment of euphoric delirium.

Arms wrapped tightly around his head, face buried deeply in his neck, she raised her head slightly and happened to see a wild parrot sitting among the fronds of a palm tree right outside the arched window, looking right at her. It was like a dream or a detail from a Latin American magic realist novel. She wondered what it meant, even though she didn't put much stock in the meaning of such things. Then the bird noticed her, squawked, and flew straight up in a burst of bright green feathers.

Green for go, she thought, just as Pete pivoted toward the bed. "Now this is a reunion . . . worth coming to . . . or at," she started in a murmur and, due to circumstances far beyond her control, finished in a squeal. They both laughed, tumbling onto the bed, Pete unleashing the full weight of his passion . . . his lifelong, true-blue crush on Cynthia, letting gravity help him have his way with her, plunging, penetrating deeper than deep . . . both crying out in one voice of longing and lust.

They ravaged each other with wild abandon . . . hot, heavy, then tender, then hot and heavy again. He was a virtuoso of his instrument. He played her with every inch of his cock, from head to shaft to root, teasing every nerve ending from the sweet high notes of her clitoris, to her G to

Do-Re-Mi spots, to the pounding, shuddering, orchestral tones
that can only emanate from within the dark recesses, beyond
the proscenium and curtains, deep inside the warm chamber
of flesh, where hot-wet-hard-soft pleasures collide, resounding
upward and outward through bliss and bone and psyche and
sighs, like lush under and overtones throbbing in unison with
natural rhythms and amplifying them beyond belief. Both
perched on the verge of climax, shaking on orgasm's edge,
Cynthia's trembling fingers crawled out of the holes they'd dug
into Pete's rock-hard ass, and reached out and around to track
down, then tease and follow his tight, slapping, bouncing balls.
They were a moving target and she strained and stretched and
finally made brief contact with an index finger, then another,
teasing his plums with a firm flutter that caused Pete to cry
out and plunge in even deeper . . . impossibly deep, impossibly
hard. This symphony of ecstasy escalated into an exquisite
crescendo, the entire composition finally breaking down into
delicious, calamitous cacophony, uncontained by mere floors
and walls, let alone open windows, echoing off the nearby
Hollywood sign, across canyon and flats . . . hanging in the
warm California air like a clarion call of deep requited desire.

Day 2, Chapter 12

Lolita was riding up Beachwood Drive when she heard someone, somewhere in the throes of passion.

Yet another somebody is having more fun than me.

She snaked through the canyon streets, winding her way up to Cynthia's house. She had jettisoned some of her anger along the way. She wasn't going to tell Cynthia off. She was looking forward to just chatting, hearing about her friend, Jack--she would have to accept that. Or at least she'd pretend she did.

She was surprised to find Tanya walking away from Cynthia's front door, sipping a cappuccino.

Tanya was just as surprised to see her.

"Well," said Lolita, dismounting the bike and moving toward her, "fancy meeting you here."

"Likewise," said Tanya.

"Really, though," said Lolita, talking now like a corny cowboy, sounding sort of funny . . . sort of intimidating, "what brings you 'round these here parts?"

"Umm, well," said Tanya tentatively. She had planned on eventually telling her Cynthia was thinking about hiring her, but feeling increasingly uncomfortable about doing it here, now. "I dropped something off for Cynthia."

"What did you drop off?" she asked, focusing in like a police interrogator on her former employee.

"Well, umm . . ." she stammered nervously, "We talked yesterday about, well, about me . . . umm . . ."

"Me umm what?"

"Well, me sort of, kind of, you know, possibly working for her."

Lolita screamed so loudly that Tanya dropped her cappuccino. Then Lolita dropped her motorcycle helmet, which bounced down the hill, possibly all the way to Franklin Avenue, a small brown cappuccino river trickling behind it.

A little higher up in the canyon, just a few blocks away, two lovers stopped what they were doing, freezing in a pose that would make the illustrator of the Kama Sutra blush.

Cynthia removed her mouth and hands from the three Pete body parts she had glommed onto. A trickle of perspiration made its way down her forehead, welling in her eyebrow.

"Did you hear that?" she asked, wiping the sweat away.

"Yup," said Pete, coming up for air and turning his head to listen——then pausing to crack the crick in his neck—— "the unmistakable wail of the Hollywood Hills coyote."

"Wait a minute," she said, sitting up straight in bed, "what time is it?"

"Who cares?" asked Pete, leisurely tickling her ass with his toe.

"I do!" she said, jumping up and running to the living room. She found her phone. It was percolating with messages. 12:43. She really had to get going. "Goddamn it! I can't believe it!"

"Hey," said Pete, walking through the room and to the kitchen. "I realize I really need to get going too. You want a quick breakfast?"

Cynthia's phone rang. Tanya.

"No, no, Pete," she said, pulling on her underwear, "hold on . . ."

"Tanya?" she asked, looking under the couch for her bra . . ." What's up? "She put the phone on speaker so she could get down and reach for the stray undergarment.

Tanya's voice was loud and panicky. "Cynthia, I am so sorry. I really screwed up. Are you in the neighborhood? I can be there in five minutes."

"Hold on, Tanya. Calm down. What's going on?"

"Well, I just dropped off my resume at your house and I bumped into Lolita. I thought she was going to kill me on your front steps."

"Lolita? What? What are you talking about? Why was she even there?" Now she was pacing, struggling with the clasp of her bra. Pete walked over, fastened it for her, kissed her neck in a gesture of comfort, and returned to the kitchen.

"Well," said Tanya, "what happened was I didn't quit, she *fired* me. But now she wants me back. And she's totally pissed at you for stealing me away."

"What? But I didn't. You called *me*. And I haven't even *hired* you yet, anyway. I was going to talk to Lolita about it first."

"I know, I know. I'm just saying that's what she *thinks*. I told her she was wrong, but she was not in a listening mood. You know how she gets. She's even *more* pissed that you're screwing Jack Stone. I guess she wanted you to set *her* up with him or something?"

"Set *her* up with him?" she asked, buttoning on her blouse. "Lolita is delusional."

Pete stuck his head out of the kitchen door. He didn't have to actually ask *are you screwing Jack Stone?* His quizzical look asked it loud and clear.

"Hold on, Tanya. Pete, I am not screwing Jack Stone."

"Not according to Lolita," said Tanya.

"Tanya!" she shrieked. "Who would know better, me or Lolita?"

"Well," said Tanya, "she knows that you were at his house yesterday and that you said he was coming on to you."

"Yeah, well, that's true," she said, looking over at Pete, who was now sitting on the floor, leaning against the wall, with a stunned look on his face. "But," she continued, "that doesn't mean I did anything about it!" She shrugged at Pete with an expression of exasperated innocence, trying to win his confidence regarding this fiasco, but he didn't look particularly convinced.

"Wait," said Tanya, deeply skeptical as well, "let me get this straight. You turned down Jack Stone? *That's* your story? Because I sort of have corroboration on it from a whole other source."

"You *what?*" blurted Cynthia. *What was she talking about?* "Why, did you talk to Jack or something?"

That did not come out right. Pete got up and left the room.

"Pete, hold on, it's not what you think."

"No, no, I didn't," said Tanya, now sounding a bit insulted that *her* credibility was being questioned. "I have this friend I went to college with. Her name is Mariana."

"Mariana? Who's Mariana?" asked Cynthia, but remembering before she finished asking. *Oh. My. God. What are the odds?*

"She works for Jack Stone. Well, she *worked* for him. She got fired yesterday too. The whole world seems to be getting fired. Mariana told me all about how you were over there, drinking and flirting and that you got her axed because you were all jealous or something."

"Me? Jealous? Of Mariana? Oh, please. Jack told me all about her. She's infatuated with him. Obsessed. I didn't get her fired. She's insane."

"So," said Tanya, "*she's* insane, *Lolita's* insane, *everyone's* insane, huh?"

"Well, if by everyone you mean those two insane people, yes!"

"Okay," said Tanya, "well, I must be insane too. I was Mariana's roommate at Brown for two years. She was the smartest girl in our class. She's beautiful, brilliant, and about the sanest person I know. Plus, why would she be going goofy over an old-guy movie star like Stone? She's had the same boyfriend since I met her and he's as brilliant and beautiful as *she* is!"

"Yeah, but she broke up with him. Believe me, girls go a little crazy when there's a bona fide movie star around."

"Yeah," said Tanya, "just like you did."

"No, like I *didn't!*"

"Right. Anyway, I'm going back to Lolita's shop. She's a little crazy too, but she calmed down and doubled my salary and is paying my health insurance. I can handle that kind of crazy. Bye."

"Wait!" said Cynthia, but Tanya had already hung up.

Pete appeared before her, dressed, with a small suitcase over one shoulder and a guitar bag over the other.

"Gotta go. I'm off to LAX."

"What? Now?"

"Yeah, I told you."

"But I didn't know it was *today!*"

"I tried to tell you. And it's a long tour. We won't swing back through the states until at least October."

"You're kidding. Pete, listen. None of that stuff on the phone was true. I mean, some of it was, but not the bad parts. I'm not seeing Jack Stone. He did sort of come on to me, but I turned him down. I turned him down because of you."

"Because of *me?* Cynthia, we just ran into each other two hours ago."

"I know, I know. It sounds stupid, but it's true. I heard you were in town and I started thinking about you."

"So, maybe you did. Listen, it was great to see you. I like you. I've always liked you. But it's a really long tour. Let's just say goodbye and we can touch base again next year. I'm a good old friend, but I can't compete with somebody like Jack Stone. In fact, I've lost a girlfriend and a wife to Jack Stone types. I am not up for that again."

"But, Pete, I'm not even *seeing* him. I promise."

"Okay, okay, I believe you. The only thing I can think of is that you could drive me to the airport. Not glamorous, but at least we can *talk*."

"Now? I can't. I've got a dinner thing. But I could maybe break it. I'd need to call. It's kind of a big deal."

"Kind of a big deal. Why, what is it?"

"It's not important."

"Really. A big deal that's not important. Let me guess: Jack Stone."

She closed her eyes and shook her head. "Yes, but . . ."

"I'm outa here," he said walking toward the door.

"But, Pete. It doesn't mean anything. It's business. He's a client. I run a dating service. He just wants me to help him find him someone."

Pete looked at her like she had lost her mind. He was beyond the end of his rope. He inhaled slowly, like he was carefully measuring the exact amount of breath he'd need to deliver his next line.

"I see," he said, "because Jack Stone can't get a date. Listen,

I take it back. I don't want to see you again. Ever. Just close the door on the way out." He quickly descended the stairs.

"Wait, no wait!" she pleaded from the landing, still determined to explain that he'd gotten it all wrong, but then, instead of crying, "Pete!" she cried, "Jack!"

Ugh.

To her, this had no significance except that they had just been *talking* about Jack, but Pete made no such assumption. He walked out the door, down the walk, and got into his car.

She cried out again and then once more as he disappeared down the hill.

That's when she really cried.

Day 2, Chapter 13

Frustrated that she still hadn't heard from her daughter about setting up a date with Dominic, and also desperate to get the scoop on her meeting with Jack Stone, she called again.

Cynthia was back home, staring out the window. How had things gone so horribly wrong? She heard her phone buzz and didn't even feel like looking at it. She figured it was Lolita and really did not want to talk to her. She knew she needed to apologize and straighten everything out. She didn't want to risk losing her best friend, but she couldn't bear it. Lolita would just have to wait. She let it buzz until it stopped.

But then it buzzed again. Someone was persistent. She knew who.

She picked up. "Mom?"

"Cindy, where have you been? I was starting to worry."

"Don't, worry, Mom, there's nothing at all to worry about," she said in a voice so gloomy it was the very definition of something a mother would worry about.

"Cindy," she said, "what is it? What happened? How did it go with Jack Stone? You know I've been dying to find out."

"Oh, that? Who cares," she said, still sounding dangerously down in the dumps.

"Who cares? Sweetie, what is going on? Was he mean to you or something? He was so nice to me at the Ivy?"

"Mom, no, he wasn't mean. I think he actually *likes* me."

"Wait, you mean *like* likes?"

"Yes, Mom, *like* likes."

"And this is what you're sounding suicidal about?"

"No, Mom! I'm feeling bad about Pete Blatt!"

"You mean that incident way back when you were kids when he threw up and had that erection while he was talking to me? Why would you all of a sudden be feeling bad about that?"

"No! Not that, Mom! I saw him! Today! I really like him, but he's leaving town!"

"Wait, I thought he just got here."

"He did, but he's leaving again. He's a musician, he's on tour!"

"Hold on. He's a musician? Musicians are very unreliable, Cindy."

"No, not him. He's not. He's still the same sexy, sweet, talented guy he was when he was a kid."

"Sexier and sweeter and more talented than Jack Stone? I'm just saying."

"Mom! I don't want to talk about it. Please, I'll call you later. I've gotta go."

"Wait, while I have you on the phone, please, look up who I chose on your site. I want you to set something up. He looks and sounds just darling. Please, make the arrangements."

"Okay, Mom, no problem," said Cynthia, at that moment really not caring who her mother wanted to go on a date with. She opened the site and without even looking, she accepted her mother's request, which had apparently already been accepted by the lucky gentleman, so now they'd both hear back that everything was set. Cynthia had designed the site to accommodate last-minute emergencies like this. It was the first time she'd used this feature and she was glad she did, because in some ways she sort of dreaded going through the process of matching up her mother. A much as she wanted to find someone for her, the process itself was a potential minefield. This was perfect. Whoever the guy was, he'd already said yes. That was *more* than half the battle. Both of them would be informed of the time and place and she, Cynthia, wouldn't need to go through the almost certainly problematic procedure. And everyone on the site had been screened thoroughly.

"Okay, Mom, done," she said, clicking off the site and settling back into her own despondent doldrums. "You'll get an email letting you know where to go. Hey, since when are you so good at navigating the internet?"

"Thanks, honey, you're a doll," Margie said, hoping her avoidance would pass unnoticed. She loved asking Cindy for help and she'd use that ploy again soon enough. "So, what are you doing tonight? Staying home, I guess, nursing your little old Pete Blatt broken heart?"

"Oh, stop it, Mom, I'm serious. He's a sweet guy. We really had a lot of fun today, before everything went to hell. But no, I'm going somewhere tonight. I have a thing."

"You have a thing. What on Earth is that? Cindy, what are you talking about? Is this why your father and I spent all that money sending you to college? So that you can speak so articulately? What the heck is a *thing*?"

"Oh, I'm going over to Steven Sternberg's house tonight. With Jack. Jack Stone. I guess Beyoncé performed last time. Don't know who will tonight. It's a benefit for something, so I guess a lot of other celebs'll be there too. Whatever. I don't really want to go."

Margie didn't say a word. In fact, the pause on the line

was so long, Cynthia was afraid her she'd had a heart attack or a stroke or had nodded off or something.

"MOM! ARE YOU THERE?!"

"Yes, dear, I'm here. You don't really want to go? YOU DON'T REALLY WANT TO GO? Tell you what. *You* stay home and watch *Celebrity Apprentice*, *Celebrity Rehab, and Dancing with the Washed-up Stars*, and I'll go on a date to Steven Sternberg's house with Jack Fucking Stone!"

Cynthia had never heard her mother used the F word. It's funny when you think about your parents being above certain behavior or language. Parents try to shelter their kids from things like swearing, but they're just people, of course they swear.

"Did you just say what I *thought* you said?" she asked her mother, smiling a bit for the first time in a couple of hours.

"You're damn right," said Mom. "People sometimes get *frustrated* with people, for fuck's sake."

"JESUS CHRIST!" screamed Cynthia, who had just noticed the time.

"What? What's so bad about me swearing once in a while? I mean, you needed to hear something that would snap you out of your ridiculous Gloomy Gusses. Did I ever tell you about the time . . ."

"Mom! I'm so sorry, but I'm late! It's 3:53! He's going to be here any minute!"

"Who, Pete Blatt?"

"No! Jack Stone! He's coming to pick me up!!!"

"*Jack Stone* is coming to *your* house to pick *you* up."

"Yes, Mom, yes!"

"And I'm supposed to feel sorry for you? *Why exactly?*"

"Never mind, Mom. Gotta go. I'm not even dressed yet!"

"Okay, but say hi to him for me."

"Mom, he doesn't remember you. He meets thousands of people!"

"But only one me. Did you ask him?"

"No, but . . ."

"No buts. I bet you a million dollars he remembers me. Ask him."

"And how would you pay up on that?"

"Just ask him!"

"Okay, but I really have to go now."

"All right, honey, but . . ."

"Really . . . have . . . to . . . go."

"BUT I WANT DETAILS!"

Click.

Day 2, Chapter 14

Cynthia quickly wrote a note——"Hi, come on up. I'll be ready in a minute."——and taped it to the front door and left the latch unlocked. She headed for the bathroom, ripped off her clothes like they were on fire, and hopped into the shower. She went into rapid-shower mode. It was like a military drill. She washed every nook and cranny like an over-caffeinated efficiency expert.

She heard a noise. Jack had arrived and he was moving around in the living room.

"Hi, Jack!" she called, "I'll be right out! Help yourself to anything, which pretty much means nothing, in the fridge!"

He didn't call back to her, so she assumed he simply couldn't hear her over the sound of the shower.

She got out of the shower and quickly dried off. She needed to get dressed, but she felt slightly weird to not at least say hello. So she put on her robe, hesitating for a moment, wishing it wasn't such an old one. It wasn't exactly in tatters, but this was Jack Major Heartthrob Fucking Stone, as her elegant mother was fond of calling him. She checked the mirror, testing her sexy smile——yes, still working——and walked out into the hallway.

He was standing near the window, facing the expanse of canyon and the flats of Hollywood beyond. He was holding a glass of wine. Although she did wonder how horrible that particular bottle of wine might be. It wasn't 2-Buck Chuck, but it was close.

"Hi, Jack, how are you?" she said.

"I'm fine, Sin," he replied, turning around, "but you can call me Max, Sin."

Good god! Max! Cynthia was so surprised by this, she recoiled in a cartoonish, totally exaggerated way, like she was overacting.

"What on Earth are you doing here?" she said. "I thought you were at some south-sea resort somewhere."

"Keyword: *were*. Or *was*, I guess. I got to thinking about you and how much I missed you, Sin."

Oh my god, how incredibly strange have the last two days been? When it comes to highly idiosyncratic, over-sexed men and me, when it rains it apparently pours.

"Ah, Max, it's great to see you and we should really grab some coffee or something, but this is not a good time. More like a very *bad* time. You can't just barge in on people."

"Hey, I didn't put the sign saying '*Come on up*' on your door."

"No, I know, but the sign was obviously meant for someone else. If it had been for you, it would have said, '*Hey, Max, cut your vacation short in freaking Fiji, hop on a plane to Los Angeles, get your ass over to Beachwood Canyon, and come on up!* 'It didn't say *that* did it?"

"I've never been a big rule follower."

"You can say that again. Listen, like I said, I am expecting someone."

"Jack Stone?"

"As it happens, yes. And I would appreciate it if you would get out of here. Now. This is really just a business meeting. It's not a big deal. But you would really help me out if you left."

"Okay, so do you always have business meetings in your bathrobe? I'm just asking. Just curious."

"Max, no. I was running late. Tell you what. Let's set a time to get together. How's early next week for you?"

"Early next week? I just traveled five thousand miles to see you."

"Yeah, well I didn't ask you to. Please."

Suddenly, there was a knock on the door.

"Hello? Cynthia?" This time it actually was Jack Stone. "Hello?"

"Hi, Jack!" she chirped.

She turned to Max. "Listen. Get out now. Go down the back way."

"You want me to sneak out the back way, like some kind of philandering backdoor man?"

Jack's footsteps getting closer.

"Yes, exactly. Exactly like that."

"Why is it such a big deal if you're just having a business meeting?"

"I don't know. It just *is*." She really *wasn't* sure why. It was partly because Max was a master of unnecessary complication and controversy. He just had a knack for messing things up. But was there something else at work here? It was called Jack and Max in the same room. And Pete, still in her head.

Footsteps on the landing.

"Forget it, Max," she said. "Just please be nice."

"Nice? When am I not nice?"

"Be *sane*. Please," she said, turning to Jack, just walking in. "Jack! You found the place!"

"I got turned around a bit, but it's such a great neighborhood to be lost in. How the heck have you been since last we met?"

He was only slightly more dressed-up than he'd been at his house. When movie stars go to big meetings with famous film directors they dress like regular people do on vacation.

"I'm fine, just fine," she said. She realized she was much more nervous here, in her house, than she had been at his. That was a dream and this was real. Reality was a lot more nerve-wracking. She realized that she hadn't introduced Max yet. "Oh! How stupid of me. Max, this is Jack. Jack, Max. He's my . . ."

"Brother," said Max, reaching out and shaking Jack Stone's hand.

"Oh, wow," said Jack. "It's a pleasure to meet you. Do you live here in L.A.?"

"Nope, no he doesn't," said Cynthia. "He's visiting. Visiting from . . ."

"Fiji," said Max.

"Wow," said Jack, "Fiji. How the heck did you end up in Fiji?"

Max smiled at him dully, making Cynthia very nervous. He was such a wild card. One couldn't possibly predict how he'd run with a situation like this. He might actually behave himself and he might go nuts.

"Fiji," he said, "Yes. How did I get there? I flew there. You know, in an airplane. Whoosh!"

Jack and Cynthia stared at him, then at each other. Jack cracked up. "Ha, ha! Cynthia, I see he has your sense of humor. Funny genes, I guess."

"Yeah," said Max, "well our dad was very funny. *Very* funny. Wasn't he, Sin?"

"Oh, sure," she said. "Hilarious."

"Listen," said Max, "I should probably go, but I just want to say that I love your movies. Well, not all of them, I mean, I bet you didn't even sit through *The Long Way Down*. Your acting was fine, but you should have sued the writer and director on that turkey."

"Really?" asked Jack. "I'm sorry you didn't like it. I wrote and directed that one."

"Well I really liked it," said Cynthia, feeling slightly nauseous.

"That's funny," said Max. "We saw it together and you hated it more than I did. *You* were the one who wanted to walk out. I mean, I did too, but you were adamant about it."

"As usual, you're remembering it all wrong," she said. "I was enjoying it. I just had the flu. I *had* to leave. Speaking of leaving, Max."

"Oh, yeah, I'm outa here. How I do go on. I'm afraid I really put my foot in it. Well, Jack, sorry about *The Long Way Down*. At least you didn't finance it, right?"

"No, actually, I *did* finance it."

"Okay, Max," said Cynthia ushering him out. "It was great to see you and have a great flight back to Fiji."

"You're leaving right now?" asked Jack, looking dubious. "Too bad. You could come with us to Steven Sternberg's house tonight."

"No," said Cynthia. "That's impossible, right, Max. You've gotta get going. Gotta catch that plane."

"Yup," said Max. "Too bad. I'm off. You know me: whoosh!"

"Goodbye, Max," said Cynthia in a voice that was positively subzero. Plus wind chill.

"So long, brother Max," said Jack.

"Bye, Sis," chirped Max heading down the stairs.

"Okay," said Cynthia, "I really need to get dressed."

"Your brother is an odd fish."

"Mentally ill is more like it."

"As I told you before, people sometimes start behaving strangely when then get around so-called celebrities. It's kind of unavoidable."

"Yeah, well he's got other problems that I don't want to go into now."

"At first I thought he was your boyfriend."

"No, no, god, no."

"Does he really live in Fiji?"

"No. He just came from there. He lives somewhere around here. At least in California. I think. He travels a lot. Not sure if he really lives *anywhere*."

"Wow. Okay, so, who's the boyfriend? The guy you turned me down for."

"Oh, yeah, him. Well, that whole thing ended today. He hates my guts. And he left town."

"Great," said Jack with a smile. "I'm kidding. That's just terrible. How could anyone hate your guts? I love your guts. Anyway, why don't you get dressed and I'll go get a bottle of wine from the car. It's a Shiraz. I don't know anything about wine really, but I have a feeling it's very good. Clint gave me a case and he does everything well. I think he might own the vineyard."

"Why do rich people always get free stuff? They're the people who can afford to *buy* it."

"I know. It's totally unfair. I'll bring up the whole case if you promise to share it when I come over."

Holy shit. Jack Stone is planning on coming over here on a regular basis all of a sudden?

"I'll get it from the car. You get dressed. Or not. I don't mind you like that."

She looked over at the mirror on the far wall. She looked

like she'd been through a category five hurricane. Her hair was a snake's nest of tangles. It had dried into an unmitigated mess.

"I'll be right back," she said.

"I was an Eagle Scout," he said. "I'm an expert at tying and untying knots."

Cynthia smiled and rolled her eyes. "I bet you're talented at a lot of things. A Jack of all trades."

"So to speak," he said, smiling back.

Day 2, Chapter 15

Upon leaving Cynthia's, Max walked down Beachwood to Franklin. He had taken a cab to Cynthia's place directly from the airport. He had absolutely nothing with him and, because he hadn't lived in Los Angeles for years, he wasn't even sure where he wanted to go or what he wanted to do next. He hadn't eaten anything other than a few peanuts and chips on the plane and he was starving. He came to a place called Hole in the Wall, a dingy bar that served dingier food. Perfect.

He sat at the bar and ordered a scotch, a beer, and a burger and contemplated life. He was aware that he was a handful for any woman. When Cynthia had abandoned him on that lonely cliff in Malibu——naked, cold, and horribly frustrated, it had really gotten to him. It was a wake-up call. He'd immediately gone on a 'round the world trip. He spent more than a month in Asia——China, Japan, Viet Nam,

Cambodia, Burma, Sri Lanka——met a lot of women and shared a laugh and a tumble with quite a few. But he missed Cynthia. He'd thought of her constantly. This wasn't new. The same thing had happened when he was married. In the throes of passion with his wife, he had called out Cynthia's name more than once and then, the last straw was when she realized he'd been carrying around a garment of Cynthia's in his suitcase for *years*, like a magical fetish, a funky piece of voodoo mojo or gris gris or something. Understandably, the wife freaked out, because, well, it was pretty freaky, and a deep insult to someone who was supposedly the love of his life. Until those clues started surfacing, his wife hadn't even heard of Cynthia, so she hadn't realized just how much more insulted she should have been when he'd named their *cat* Cynthia and for months had been calling out: "Cynthia! Here, pussy, pussy! Oh, Cynthia! Where's my sweet little pussy?" His wife put that particular two plus two together moments after she'd busted him on the suitcase-talisman thing, so in the middle of kicking him out, she chased him down the front walkway to *re*-kick him out, slamming him hard on the back of the head with a very potent kitty litter tray and depositing the cat itself at his feet as well, since——hello——she was allergic anyway, and screaming for all of Santa Barbara to hear, "And take your goddamn pussy with you!"

He'd gone straight back to Cynthia, meeting her at Shutter's in Santa Monica, and everything was right in his world, until it all went to hell again. He knew he was to blame, at least somewhat, but he also felt that he was a victim of the whims of his goddamn penis. He chuckled to himself: *Damn you, penis! Damn you all to hell!*

While traveling, he had done a lot of thinking——on beaches, mountaintops, and other gorgeous, yet clichéd, locations——where travelers seek answers. Along the way he often laughed at himself because suddenly he felt he was living in some kind of chick flick or piece of pop-philosophy, like *Eat, Pray, Love*, a book and movie he'd never seen, but still had mocked incessantly. But there he was——a womanizer of the first degree going soft, actually feeling something for someone in a way he never had——halfway around the world from that very object of affection.

He had finished the scotch and beer by the time the food came, so he ordered another round. There was a guy at the other end of the bar who looked like he'd been drinking since the place opened. Good god, he looked bad. But then Max caught a glimpse of himself in the mirror and he didn't look too much better. Less likely to end up in the Hollywood drunk tank tonight, perhaps, but in a way, just as desperate.

He wanted Cynthia. He needed Cynthia. She was his

salvation. He knew that now. He was looking for the bartender, wanting one more drink, when someone tapped his shoulder.

"Excuse me," said a lovely woman dressed completely in red, carrying a noticeably dented motorcycle helmet, "are you Max by any chance?"

She looked vaguely familiar to him, but he had no idea why. The experience of traveling is disorienting. His mind was a swirl of past and distant past. He had no idea if he'd met this person twenty years ago or yesterday, in Fiji or Timbuktu.

"Don't tell me," he said. "It'll come to me."

"We went to a costume party together once," she said. "Last Halloween. The beach."

"Wait. Cynthia's friend! The dog person!"

"I don't normally answer to 'dog person'. If you want me to come when you call, try Lolita."

"Lolita! Of course! How could I forget? Lo. Lee. Tah. So scandalous, so Nabokovian, so . . ." He looked straight into her cleavage in a way that only a bold man made bolder by drink would even try. "I'm having a flashback involving olives? No, grapes . . . and those beautiful tits. Am I right? Malibu? You know, it's funny. I was just thinking about that night."

"Thinking of me or that horrible Cynthia?"

"Hold on, wait. Cynthia is horrible now? But she's your

friend, right?"

"Was. Well, I'm pretty pissed at her, but I suppose I'll get over it eventually."

"Oh, good, because, let me tell you a secret. I'm in love with her."

"Get out," she said, pushing against his shoulder.

"Nope . True love. But she doesn't really know yet. She's running around with that stupid movie star. You know, the stupid one from that stupid movie. We walked out. Sin hated it. But now she says she liked it, but she's just kissing up to the stupid movie star. Probably a lot more than kissing up, I bet."

"Really. Listen, Max. I think you've got to get her back."

"Yeah," he said. "And, funny thing. I happen to know where they're going tonight. Steven Sternberg's bash. Wanna go?"

"Wow," said Lolita. "I am *so* up for that, it hurts. Okay, okay, Max. Why don't we just head over there?" She put her arm around him and spun him slowly on the barstool.

"Sounds wonderful, Lo . . . lee . . . tah," he replied, sliding to a standing position and steadying himself by holding her hands and facing her. "Hey, I wonder if they have any grapes here."

"No, Max, bars don't sell grapes unless they're fermented," she said, walking arm-in-arm with him out onto Franklin Avenue. "I thought you were in love with Cynthia anyway."

"Oh, I am, I am. I'm *completely* in love with *her*. But," he said, pausing to kiss both of her breasts, "I'm *partially* in love with *you*."

This could have insulted Lolita, but she just laughed and took it in stride. "I'm sure there are some parts of you that I would like too, Max." She kissed him on the lips, slapped his butt, and loaded him onto her hot pink Vespa.

"I've been known to speed," she said, "so hang on!" But he hardly needed to. For one thing, when you load two fairly large people onto a Vespa, especially *this* Vespa, you're not about to speed anywhere. That was why it was pretty obvious that the fervor with which Max wrapped his arms around Lolita's chest was much more inspired by lust and liquor than safety.

Day 2, Chapter 16

After polishing off that bottle of Shiraz, an entire box of crackers, and a large block of Vermont cheddar cheese——Jack was enthralled that she had it, having spent summers as a kid in the Green Mountain State and being firm in the resolve that cheese should be sharp and *yellow*, not bland and *orange*, like some Wisconsin cheese-heads would have you believe——they were ready to roll. They had eaten the equivalent of a fairly large dinner, so the wine had little effect on either of them.

They walked down to his extremely dingy sports car. It needed a paint job and was absolutely filthy. But it had a familiar shape.

"What is this car and did you drive it through a category five shit storm on the way over?"

"Ha. It's an Astin Martin db5."

"A Bond car, right?"

"*The* Bond car. For the first few films, anyway."

"His were cleaner."

"Yeah, well, Bond didn't have to evade paparazzi. I go anywhere I want. Some of my friends never leave their compounds. I decided a long time ago I wasn't going to live like that. I go places and do things. As long as I keep moving, don't linger in any one spot too long. At the movies? Get in fast and get out faster. Pinkberry? Go, go, go, and eat it on the road. I'm like a one-man commando unit. You'll see. I don't whine about it, because it's actually kind of fun. And I don't ever wash or paint my cars. From the outside it's a beater, but it drives like one of the world's great automobiles, because it is."

"You are smarter than you look," she said, buckling her seatbelt.

He turned to her and made a goofy dumb-guy face, before pulling away from the curb and gently accelerating, then coasting down to Franklin. He turned right at the bottom of the hill and headed west, picking up speed, hitting all the lights just right, then up Cahuenga Boulevard, winding through Cahuenga Pass, home of the Hollywood Bowl and Whitley Heights, the "Beverly Hills" of the silent era——

"Valentino lived right up there!" she called out, pointing,

and Stone replied, "I know! And W.C. Fields. And Harlow!" She loved that he was a true movie fan. She had met plenty of movie people who weren't, which she could barely believe. He sped up, traveling parallel to the 101 freeway, over the bridge to Woodrow Wilson Drive, then Mulholland, the greatest road in the world, well, one of the greatest, where he really opened up, snaking along the spine of the Santa Mountain Range. She loved that he loved this, because she did too. It was wonderful and wild. Even more so in this car.

"The sunset's going to be an award winner," he said. "And I want to get to my favorite lookout in time."

"Ahh," she said, fingernails digging into the armrest.

He wasn't kidding. They turned a corner and came to a break in the trees, revealing a sky that had considerably reddened since they left her house.

She couldn't see the speedometer, but she didn't want to know anyway. He crossed over Laurel Canyon, again hitting the light perfectly. How did he do that? Then, around past the dog park——the best dog park in L.A., and then, the Mulholland Lookout up on the left, the Hollywood side.

He pulled in quickly, sending up a cloud of dust, then hit the brakes and skidded with some drama but more precision into the only parking spot partially sheltered by trees.

They sat there as the dust settled. "The view from my

house is *good* . . . from yours too, but this one's incredible. I stop here all the time. Sometimes if the traffic is congested, I'll pull over and just wait."

"Yeah," she agreed. "I love this road. When I was a teenager, this was a very popular necking spot."

"Still is," he said with a smile. "Oh, my god. Look at that."

The sunset was kicking into high gear. Red and orange were breaking over the contours of the most westerly canyons. Coldwater, Benedict, and beyond. Blinding orange and red reflected off the glass edifices of Westwood and Century City, leaving long shadows in their wake.

"The ocean looks like it's made of silver," he said, putting his hand on her shoulder.

Uh-oh, she thought. *Here it comes.* Her defenses were seriously weakened now. Pete hated her and she hated Max. She wondered how she had been so infatuated with him for so long. His selling points were really very badly trounced by Jack's. And Jack was so much less arrogant about his talents and about everything, really. It was incredibly hard not to like Jack. He hadn't overtly come on to her since back at his house——not counting this little shoulder touch——he had been wooing her in a million different more subtle ways. It was like he wasn't doing anything at all, yet he was, and she was aware of it. She also appreciated it. She liked that he had the patience to let it unfold.

She touched his hand and he touched her knee. The sunset's glow filled the car with yellow-orange light, somehow making him look even better, nature's Photoshop.

"Look," he said. The sky was peaking. The spectrum of colors had reached an almost unbelievable degree of brilliance and variation. It was beyond postcard perfect. It was the kind of sappy movie moment that she would undoubtedly ridicule as saccharine hogwash if she were watching it in the local multiplex, but here, there was nothing phony about it. It was breathtaking and profound.

"I know what I told you before," she said. "But it would be a crime to be with a person in a situation like this, and not kiss that person."

He laughed softly, the light on his face moving from red to purple and blue, as the sun dipped into the sea. He turned and moved in closer and kissed her softly, then deeply.

Somehow he had done it. He had gotten her to want and ask for this without doing much at all. She felt manipulated, but not terribly unhappy about it. She tasted the wine on his lips and felt it a little in her head.

Their movements were seriously restricted inside the sports car, but it didn't matter. They weren't looking for all-out lovemaking at that moment anyway. Simple gestures and soft touches carried more than their weight in sensual impact. She moved a hand to his thigh, he, one to her breast . . . and just kept them there, not moving, just sensing, their deep kisses transporting them over the Los Angeles sprawl below, *like a couple in a Marc Chagall painting,* she thought. Apparently they were operating under Chagall's laws of physics.

She felt his hand under her blouse and had absolutely no recollection of him untying the elaborate laces that held it together. He wasn't kidding about the Boy Scout stuff. And just as his lips touched the skin adjacent to the laced upper hem of her bra, and his tongue found its way under that hem . . .

Knock! Knock! Knock! A flash of light. A flashlight, in fact. Someone was at the window on her side.

"Open up!"

"Jesus!" said Cynthia and Jack simultaneously. He instantly covered her up and lowered the window.

"Yes, officer?"

"Just get out of the car."

So they did. They readjusted their clothing as much as possible and stood up, the bright headlights of the cruiser in their eyes.

"What seems to be the problem, sir?" asked Jack in a completely calm tone, not riled in the slightest, despite the fact that on top of everything, Cynthia at least noticed that he had a distinct circus tent happening in his trousers.

Cynthia squinted into the glare and saw that beyond the cop there were other people and other cars. Some had cameras.

"Nothing," said the officer, "we just get some wild kids up here. Can I see an I.D. please?"

"Sir," said Cynthia, "my license is in my purse. In the car." She was always fairly paranoid when she got stopped by a cop——who isn't——but thinking about her purse also reminded her of her phone and the fact that she still had a bunch of details to attend to for tonight's dates. The day had *so* slipped away. Pete, Lolita, Tanya, Max, Jack. What on Earth? She was suddenly full of anxiety about everything. It had been a wonderful afternoon with Jack, but this last turn of events just made her realize how she had let time get away from her. She must have looked a little freaked out. She really couldn't go any further with Jack. She needed to focus more on Second Acts and less on the heat of the moment. No matter how hot the moment was.

"That's okay, lady," said the cop, "his will be enough."

Jack handed over his license and the cop held it up to the light. He paused and moved super close, like he was reading braille with his nose. Then he looked at Jack and back at the license. Then he shook his head and smiled.

"No shit. I can't believe I didn't recognize you, Mr. Stone.

Sorry, it's just so dark. What are you doing up here, anyway? Wait," he said, apparently finally noticing their generally disheveled appearance, and smiling again, "Never mind."

A couple of camera flashes went off and the cop turned around.

"Get the hell outa here! What's the matter with you, anyway? Everyone needs to do some making out at a beautiful Mulholland lookout sometimes! I did it when *I* was in high school! Get the hell outa here right now and I won't give you all tickets!"

"Tickets for what?" asked one pissed-off paparazzi.

"I don't know, for being a stupid a-hole?!" said the cop.

The photographers got back into their cars, but not before snapping a few more photos and muttering a few more complaints.

"Thanks," said Jack. "You, sir, are a hero."

"No problem, man. I love your work. Except *The Long Way Down*. I walked out on that."

"He directed that one," said Cynthia, trying hard not to laugh, which only made her and Jack burst out laughing harder.

"Yeah," said Jack. "It was kind of a clunker."

"Sorry, man, I don't know why I even said that," said the cop. "I didn't see the whole thing. It might have gotten better."

Then all three of them laughed.

"This is weird," said the cop. "Can I maybe get an autograph for my wife?"

Jack happily signed the only piece of paper the officer could find--a blank Los Angeles moving violation ticket.

"There you, go," he said. "In triplicate!"

They all laughed and said goodbye. Then Jack pulled out onto Mulholland and they continued winding their way west.

"Jack," said Cynthia, "I just realized I really have to make some calls and answer some emails. Don't mind me. I'll do it while you drive."

"Good, great," he said, "Otherwise I'd be tempted to stop at the next lookout."

"I know," she said, "that was kind of an abruptus interuptus."

"Yeah, well, the night is young," he said.

And so they wound their way along the ridge, finally descending into Bel Air and to his house.

They entered the house and were greeted happily by Scarlet O'Hara, who desperately needed to be let out to pee and then eat.

Cynthia sat on the couch, finishing up some final arrangements, reassuring one client here, another there, a third who had come down with the flu and had to reschedule.

Donald Griffin O'Brien, the café guy, had called to say an employee had called in sick and that he would be late for his date with Adriana Gomez, but that she was fine with it and asked him to just come up to the Casbah whenever he was ready. Which did not sound half bad. And then Cynthia noticed something. Something she should have noticed a whole lot sooner.

Marjorie Amas was paired off with Dominic Orlando. What the hell! How did this happen? And then she remembered exactly how it happened. She had taken the short cut. She had simply okayed their match-up because they had already pre-approved each other. This was the first time she'd ever used that feature of the website and this was the result. Dominic Orlando, serial womanizer, with *her mother?*

She called her mom. Ringing . . . ringing.

She didn't pick up. "Mom. Call me. Now."

She got up and paced around Stone's gorgeous living room. It was beautiful in a whole different way at night. The twinkling lights of Hollywood had replaced the natural vista from earlier. But it was still amazing.

Mom, call back. Call back.

She really didn't have a sense of the depth of Dominic's depravity. She liked him, he was a good friend, but who knows what anyone becomes when sex is thrown into the mix? She couldn't imagine that he was dangerous, but he might be a bit kinky. We were talking about her MOM, after all.

She called again. *Ringing . . . ringing.* "Mom!"

Stone came into the room.

"What's happening? Is there a problem?"

"Oh, it's just that it turns out my mother is on a date with a sex maniac, that's all."

"Wow. How did *that* happen?"

"Well, they did it through my site. I mean, the guy is a friend of mine, but he's not the kind of guy you want hanging around your mom. He's totally girl crazy."

"I'm pretty girl crazy."

"Yeah, I know, but . . ."

"But what? If she's anything like you, she'll be fine."

Cynthia thought about that. Maybe he was right. I mean, Dominic really was a nice guy. As long as Mom didn't let him out of her sight while she was with him, he probably wouldn't cheat on her *during* dinner.

"You're upset," said Jack. "And tense. All worked up. You need to relax."

"I can't relax," she said. "I can't stop thinking about her."

"Sit back down. I'll rub your back a bit. Then we'll take off for Steven's house."

She did what he said. She really didn't think it would help, but pacing certainly wasn't either.

He rubbed her neck and shoulders with skill that no masseuse had ever exhibited. She suspected it was partly his technique and partly that he was simply Jack Stone. It was remarkable. He rubbed her head too, applying pressure at the temples and forehead, seeming to squeeze the anxiety right into thin air. She started to nod off . . . she was suddenly beyond relaxed. It felt like everything in her life stopped spinning and all that existed were his fingers and her skin and nerves beneath them. He was a virtuoso.

He moved in and kissed her shoulder, collarbone, then earlobe. She instantly felt warm. It was like he'd started a fire in the fireplace or the house itself was in flames. "Jack," she said, touching his face tenderly with her fingertips, then pushing softly but with conviction, sending the clear message that he should stop. "Shouldn't we get going?"

Day 2, Chapter 17

Lolita had thought the Vespa's gas tank was full, but she was sorely mistaken. Max was now pushing the scooter along Sunset Boulevard, while she sat and steered. The traffic was Friday-night heavy. More than one speedster living out a Mario Andretti fantasy honked his horn at them, Max reacting by using every swear word he knew and some he made up on the spot. Lolita suddenly remembered the brandy flask in her purse.

"You are the sexiest St. Bernard I have ever met," said Max, taking a swig and pushing onward.

"Woof," she said, whipping him with a branch she'd snagged from a nearby willow. "You're a pretty cute sled dog yourself."

"Woof," he said.

Lolita, being Lolita, just trying to keep the conversation flowing, divulged the Maximillian Schell "little pink Vespa" anecdote and after that, Max would not stop talking and even singing about it.

Nothing could be finer,
Than to push your pink vaginer,
In the morn-or-or-ning.

Nothing could be sweeter,
Than your Vespa when I meet her,
In the morn-or-or-ning.

"Again," she said, "Just checking. I thought you were in love with *Cynthia*."

"Again, I *am*," he said, "I'm still only partially in love with you, but the number of your parts which contribute to that love is *growing*."

"Got it," she said, whipping him again.

This stretch of Sunset was not exactly lousy with gas stations. They were coming up to 26th Street and Lolita suggested heading off course to Brentwood, where she knew there was a station on the corner of San Vicente, but Max insisted they keep forging west to the Palisades. "Go west, young woman!" he kept saying. He had a knack for keeping his chin up during times of stress. He didn't care how far he had to push, he would not go out of his way, goddammit.

Then something a tad unusual happened. Lolita looked into the small rear view mirror and noticed a small, frantic dog gaining on them from behind. Oh, my god: Wilfredo.

"Stop!" she screamed, leaping off the scooter, running against traffic to her baby, and scooping him up in her arms.

"Wilfredo! What are you doing here?!"

He licked her face and neck as she carried him back to the scooter. He was unbelievable happy to see her.

"Good god," said Max. "Do you know all dogs everywhere? Are you like the human ambassador to the worldwide canine community or something?"

"Max, this is *my* dog. Somehow he found me, despite the fact that I left Beverly Hills early this afternoon, went to the Hollywood Hills, then came back out, past my neighborhood, and he *found* me! He must have been on my trail all day!"

"I've been hot on your tail all day," said Max.

"Max!" she said, slapping him on the chest, "Listen. Now that we're moving kind of slow, no offense, he caught up with us. He's a super dog."

"Wow," said Max. "This is turning into a three dog night. Sled dog, St. Bernard, and Wilfredo-edo-edo, the Wonder Chihuahua-wah-wah-wah!"

Max pushed his face up close to the face of Wilfredo,

who sniffed and licked him all over, from nose, to eyes to ears and back around again. Max made no attempt to wipe off his face. In fact, while this was going on, Max was scratching Wilfredo behind his ears and rubbing his belly.

This was duly noted by Lolita. "So," she said, "you're a dog lover?"

"Oh, please," he said. "Are you kidding? Me and dogs go way back. That whole *man's best friend* thing is no joke, you know. It's only been going on for fifteen thousand years or so."

Wilfredo dove back into Max's neck, working his tongue like an aardvark hunting ants.

"Wilfredo is happy to hear that," said Lolita. "I am too."

"Well, good," said Max. "I hope you're equally happy to hear me say *onward!*"

"Yes, onward!" repeated Lolita, remounting the scooter——now with Wilfredo clamped happily between her thighs. Max pushed on toward the Palisades, singing verse after lewd verse about Lolita's lady bits.

Nothing could be better,
Than to be inside your sweater,
In the morn-or-or-ning.
Nothing could be nicer,
Thank to shag you once or twicer,
In the morn-or-or-ning.

Lolita and Max were laughing now. This was turning into the best vehicle malfunction ever. Max didn't bother trying to come up with a chorus. He just sang another verse:

Oh . . . you can sing the chorus,
While I nibble your clitoris,
In the morn-or-or-ning.

Lolita screamed at that one. Max could make bad rhymes forever. Pretty soon she joined in:

Serve me up some strudel,
With your cock-a-doodle-doodle,
In the morn-or-or-ning.

Max literally fell down laughing. He landed on the soft grass near the entrance of Will Rogers State Park. Lolita and Wilfredo joined him. Wilfredo licked Max's face again while the two humans laughed it out.

"I don't even care if we *make* it to the Palisades," said Lolita.

"Hold on," said Max, grabbing Wilfredo playfully and holding him at arm's length. "Never ever say that. Don't abandon hope! We'll make it to the promised land!"

"We shall!" she cried, getting back with the program.

They leaped up and soon he was pushing and singing

again. The next verse was so filthy even Wilfredo may have blushed.

Day 2, Chapter 18

Cynthia and Jack got back into his car at 7:15. He had put on a jacket and white shirt, but jeans and no tie. "I really only wear one for awards shows."

They headed down the front way, the south side, of Bel Air, to Sunset Boulevard and headed west. The Friday night traffic was heavy.

"If you don't mind," she said, "this has to be another working trip for me to make sure all's well in date-land."

She called her mom. Voice mail. "Hi, Mom, just checking in, making sure you're all set for tonight. Okay, give me a call." She hung up.

She sat and thought for a moment before calling her mother again.

"Hi, Mom, I just saw that you're seeing my old friend Dominic. He's a really nice guy and a whole lot of fun. I just wanted to warn you. Even though he says he is, I'm not completely convinced he's serious about looking for a long-term relationship. Okay. Call me. Bye."

"Wow," said Jack, "still concerned, huh."

"Yeah, well. The guy she's seeing . . . I don't know . . . he works at Marmont. He's kind of a . . ."

"Wait," said Jack, his head snapping toward her. "Are you talking about Orlando? Dominic Orlando?"

"Yeah, why? Do you know him?"

"Everyone knows him. I mean women know him a lot better than men. But, wow."

Cynthia called her mother again. Ringing, ringing . . .

"Cindy?" said her mother with a tone drenched in concern, which Cynthia immediately picked up on.

"Mom," she said, "are you all right? I never should have let you choose Dominic. He's really not right for you. I'll call him and we can reschedule something for next week with someone else. This is my fault. I'm so sorry."

Long pause. Then laughter. Two people. Her mother was on speaker with a familiar, deep, Italian-accented male.

"Cynthia, my dear," laughed Dominic, "we've had a couple of drinks and are already on the way to dinner. Listen, I like-a your mother and she like-a me. Right, Margie?"

"You're telling me, you Sicilian stallion, you."

Cynthia could not believe her ears.

"Cindy, honey," her mother continued, "Dominic has told me all about his history." Then she giggled, "I told him history was always my favorite subject."

She and Dominic burst into laughter. It was so loud, in fact, that even though Cynthia's phone was *not* on speaker, Jack totally got what was going on. He and Cynthia looked at each other and rolled their eyes.

Her mom continued, "Look, honey. I know you are looking for something long-lasting and that's great. But I'm really not. I'm looking for a good time. Dinner, some laughs, who knows. Anyway, you really don't have to worry about Dominic or me. He's a gentleman and even if he gets a little bit less gentlemanly later, I'll tell you a secret." She brought her voice down to a whisper, but the kind of whisper designed for everyone to hear anyway, "I won't mind. In fact, I'm very much looking forward to it."

Jack turned to Cynthia and smiled, shaking his head in mock judgment. "Crazy kids."

"Yeah," said Cynthia.

"What, honey?" asked Cynthia. "I can't hear you too well. We're in a canyon. Hello?"

Cynthia smiled, realizing that this was the *good* kind of mother-daughter role reversal, where the daughter suddenly feels the kind of letting-go the mother had felt years earlier. She knew that later, as her mother aged, there'd be plenty of the other kind. Knowing that made her appreciate this moment. A lot. Her mother could take care of herself. And so what if Dominic turned into a no-strings-attached one-night stand? It would have to be fun. He was fun *without* sex. And he certainly had satisfied plenty of customers over the years. Who was Cynthia to stand in the way of her mother's happiness?

"Okay," she said, "Have fun, Mom. And you treat her right, Dominic. I know where you work."

"Okay, Cindy!" said Marjorie.

"Bye-bye," chirped Dominic. "We can't hear you too good. I'm a-going through a tunnel!"

"Wheeze!" squealed Margie as the phone cut off.

"Oh my god," said Jack. "I thought I was bad."

"No," said Cynthia. "They're going through an *actual* tunnel. That double entendre was unintentional." She thought about what she just said for about two seconds and said, "No, you're right. Totally intentional. Oh my god, I don't want to think about this. Back to work." She returned to checking and writing messages to other clients.

Jack weaved around some slowpoke drivers and realized they were avoiding something . . . a man pushing something along the shoulder. Jack craned his neck as they flew by.

"Hey, Cynthia," he said, accelerating up the hill into the Palisades, "wasn't that Max, your brother, back there?"

"Back where?" asked Cynthia, looking up and around.

"He was pushing a scooter or something. With a hot girl and a little dog."

"No," she said, looking at him like he had lost his mind. "That was definitely not Max. He's gotta be on his way back to Fiji by now."

Day 2, Chapter 19

By the time the happy little Max-Lolita-Wilfredo team rolled into the Shell station in the pristine downtown section of the Pacific Palisades, they weren't so happy. Max was exhausted and Lolita was tired of his singing.

"Oh my god, I've lost my wallet," said Max.

"Wilfredo!" scolded Lolita, opening her purse and of course producing the filched item. "Sorry, he's a compulsive thief."

"No problem," said Max, rubbing Wilfredo's chin, "I'm just glad it's not lost. Onward!"

Lolita really appreciated Max's good natured enthusiasm. He seemed to effortlessly rebound from setbacks.

Once they filled the tank and started puttering along again, they both felt a whole lot better. Having an operating motor vehicle——something usually so taken for granted——suddenly felt like a super power.

They sped off toward the Sternberg estate, Max singing again, and Lolita actually liking it again, especially with his arms locked around her chest again. Wilfredo was grinning, his huge triangular ears catching the wind like little furry spinnakers.

Lolita had said from the beginning that she had been to the Sternberg house so she knew where it was, but actually finding it was easier said than done. She cut up one hill, absolutely positive she was almost there, only to come to a dead end at a water filtration plant, possibly the only ugly location in the entire town. Desolate, crumbling, it felt like they'd taken a turn into a rural slum despite the fact there wasn't a slum of any kind within thirty miles of there.

"Fantastic, Miss GPS," said Max, chuckling. "Why did I have a feeling this would happen?"

"Watch me, sled dog. I'll find it."

She circled around the gravelly end-of-the-road and dipped back down the hill to Sunset. She realized that they must have passed Sternberg's street when they were walking into town. She was almost sure.

As soon as she zipped up Amalfi Drive, she was completely positive. "Almost there," she called back to Max.

"How are you going to recognize the place?" he asked.

"Oh, believe me, I'll know."

And she was right. She remembered it was the last house, on the very top of the hill, with panoramic ocean views that went on forever. It also helped that the street was jammed with luxury cars and black-and-white vested valets. Everything except searchlights.

She pulled her little pink Vespa up behind a gigantic black hummer, out of which stepped a couple she recognized but could not identify off hand. "I wish Peterson made a field guide for celebrities," she said.

"Yeah," laughed Max. "Like a bird book. An odd-bird book. 'Oh, look. A red-breasted Amanda Seyfried nuthatch!'"

"A yellow-bellied Woody-Harrelson woodpecker!" she whispered, but then, noticing a valet with a clipboard greeting the couple enthusiastically, checking their names off his list, blurted, "Max! How are we going to get in there? We don't have an invitation. How did we not even think of this?"

"Maybe *you* didn't think of it," said Max. "No problem. I'll handle it."

"What do you mean, handle it?"

The valet approached them, looking at the scooter, then at Wilfredo. "Name?" he asked suspiciously.

"Hi," said Max, sliding off the seat and reaching over to shake his hand. "I'm Max Ramsey and this is Lolita. She's more of a one-name type. I'm actually Mrs. Sternberg's broker. I've been traveling, so I don't actually have an invitation, but I'm quite sure I'm on the list. I always am. It's kind of automatic at this point."

The valet looked down, flipping through pages. "Oh, yes, here we are," he said, checking the name with his red pen. "Go right in. There's a shuttle if you want it. Otherwise, just stay on the path and wind around through the woods. You can't miss the house."

They chose to walk, Max taking Lolita's arm in his, she holding Wilfredo like a furry football, following a bunch of other well-healed guests like a wedding procession up the steep walk.

Lolita looked at Max out of the corner of her eye and spoke in a murmur. "What the heck? How did you cook up *that* story? Who is the real Max Ramsey and what if he actually shows up?"

"News, flash, Miss GPS, I am Max Ramsey. I don't work as a broker much anymore——just for favorite clients."

"But what was that *Mrs.* Sternberg thing? You're only her broker, not his?"

"Yeah, well, he has a whole team, a whole *company*, working for him. I help her with her discretionary stuff. We have been old friends for a long time. Don't mention it to Steven, by the way. He doesn't technically know about it. I knew her before he did."

"You mean . . ." began Lolita.

"Yes," said Max. "In every sense. Not anymore, though. Water under the bridge. Maybe don't tell Cynthia either." They were passing one of the smaller buildings on the estate, a large single-family house to most people.

"That's his home office," said Lolita. "I got a tour of it way back when. But wait a minute, how come you didn't even know how to *get* here if you're always on the list?"

"I've been invited many times, but never came. I've been to the place in the Hamptons a bunch, but never, you know, when he was around."

"Right," she said.

They crested the hill and came to the main house, which looked more like a small, modern museum——actually, more like a *medium*-sized museum. It was perched on a parcel of land hovering above the ocean. To the right was a sparkling pool filled with frolicking, half-naked, gorgeous people. It was a Hollywood cliché, but a very, very attractive one. Their perfect bodies were busting out of their perfect bathing suits. It was so much sexier than nudity, Lolita had to restrain herself from just leaping in, clothes, dog, and all.

The expanse of blue sea and sky was Hollywood make-believe beautiful. The moment reminded Lolita of something, and then, when she noticed James Cameron standing nearby, chatting up a semicircle of rapt sycophants, it came to her. Dicaprio was holding Winslet as she spread her "wings" and soared above the waves on the prow of the ship in *Titanic*. Being on Sternberg's lawn was like flying.

"Max," she said, feeling a bit out of place, "I think I need a drink."

"Now you're talking," he said, heading for the bar. "I shall return." Wilfredo leaned in Max's direction as he left. Lolita tightened her grip on him and scratched his head. He really did seem to be attached to Max.

She surveyed the party, looking for Cynthia and Jack, or at least Sternberg. She did see a number of other celebrities, some of whom brought their dogs into her shop, or at least had their dogs brought in. She had met several of them before, but it was still thrilling to see them in social setting . . . in the wild. Emma Stone was standing with some hot guy she didn't recognize. *Oh, to have that field guide*, she laughed to herself. A small band of musicians played quiet, but exquisitely grungy blues over near the edge of the lawn where the land dropped off into nothingness. Lolita, a little afraid of heights, hoped to hell the drummer wouldn't forget himself, pull some kind of wacky Keith Moon-ism and hurl himself backwards off the cliff.

She looked back over to where Max had muscled his way up to a beautiful young barmaid. They were laughing. She was amazed at how fast Max charmed people. He had certainly charmed *her*. She'd gotten the distinct impression that she had done the same to him. Cynthia could have her Jack Stone. Max was hers, for the moment anyway.

And then she saw Mrs. Sternberg, AKA Molly Hannigan, a famous actress in her own right, walking across the lawn, making a beeline for Max.

She looked slightly agitated, glancing from side to side, as she approached him from behind and tapped him hard on the shoulder.

Max smiled when he saw her, but his smile disappeared almost immediately as they talked. She was gesticulating and clearly intent on conveying something important. Lolita was instantly jealous of Hannigan, even though Max had told her their affair was over. This was like watching a scene in a movie unfold. Wilfredo was watching it intently too. Lolita turned her head, taking in a sweeping view of the property, hoping for Max's sake that Sternberg wouldn't come upon them.

Day 2, Chapter 20

Cynthia and Jack had arrived at the party much earlier, but they'd gone straight into the house. Cynthia had found a quiet corner to check her phone. She had a couple of noteworthy voicemails.

Merriweather: *Beep.* "Cynthia, this Daryl is a riot. He's certainly the funniest trial attorney I've ever met. He told me an anecdote that has movie written all over it. We're back at his place writing the treatment right now. I'll get it over to Ryan Gosling tomorrow. It's a perfect fit. Speaking of which, you must be a matchmaker *and* a talent agent. Anyway, just wanted to say thanks. Oh, and thanks for dealing with the babysitter. And for finding one who's willing to stay late. I might call and ask her to stay the night. Thanks again. Bye."

Okay, one from Roger: Beep. Great call on the restaurant

change. One question. What kind of love spells are you casting anyway? Our chemistry is so perfect we literally kissed before we travelled the seventeen steps from her front door to my car. That has never happened to me. We're already finishing each other's sentences, for god's sake. Gotta go. And I don't mean leave. Adios."

Beep. "Hello, Cynthia," someone whispered. "Pick up, pick up, darlin'." Obviously Donald Griffin O'Brien. "I don't know what the hell is happenin' around here. This Casbah place is beyond a trip. This Adriana has me mummified. I'm drenched in all kinds of oils and vinegars or somethin', like I'm about to be served up to a bunch of bloody cannibals. And it's as hot as summer vacation on Venus in here."

Cynthia laughed, but was slightly concerned. She wasn't completely confident that Adriana had his best interest at heart.

"I'm lying on my back in some kind of fantasy Hobbit forest with an erection the size of Carrickfergus Castle. And all wrapped up like Boris Karloff meets Christo meets Ron Feckin' Jeremy. Not to mention my Blarney Stones. They're basted and marinated and ready to feckin' burst. Not sure what's coming next, but I have the distinct impression it's going to be me. Jesus, Mary, and Joseph, Cynthia, she's sexy. I've seen her around the neighborhood, but never up close, in her element here, wearin' you know, next to nothin', just an almost invisible robe. Wait . . . here she comes. Oh, look, she's lost the robe now. Oh, hello, darlin', so what's next on the program?"

Cynthia listened carefully, hoping beyond hope that the next sounds she heard were happy ones.

"Hello, Cynthia, it's Adriana. You're just in time for the unwrapping."

"Oh, yes, the unwrapping," said Donald, sounding simultaneously elated and a bit terrified. "Oh, and look, you're using your teeth to do it. Watch it, now that's a sensitive area, dear. Oh, Jesus, you've got a talented tongue, my dear. Oh, Jesus. God. Fuck. Jesus. Fuck. Oh. Oh. Oh. Oh. Oh. Oh. Oh."

"Okay, baby," she said with some effort in her voice, "I'm climbing aboard now. Wait, wait, hold it, hold it . . . I said, hold it, baby . . . ahh . . . ahh . . . ahhhhhh . . . dios mio . . . ahhhhh . . ."

"Oh . . ."

"Ah . . ."

"Oh . . ."

"Darlin', maybe we should hand up the phone. Don't you think this next part is just slightly private?"

"You're right, baby. This part *is* private. That's why they call it a *private part*. But I'm, you know, letting you in on my private things. But please, por favor, Donald, baby, sit up and coma mi chichis. My breasts. They are mucho jealous of my coochie-coochie coño. My pussy. My pussy is purring. Pero mi chichis are so sad, so lonely. Poor chichis. Oh, si, si . . . mucho mas mejor. But now I change my mind. Mi coño wants eating. To be eaten. Like a taco, sweetie. Do they do the 69 in Ireland? Porque mi tongue is wanting your hard, hard burrito, my baby. Please, my baby. Si, baby, si . . ."

"OH. OH. OH."

Click.

Oh. My. God. Wait. Oh, goodie. Diego.

Beep. "Cynthia, you were not kidding about this Tatiana woman. I guess I've never really seen a gymnast up close. She did a walkover——you know one of those backward cartwheely things——in the middle of the parking lot at Valentino. She was wearing a long white dress. You know that amazing picture of Martha Graham in that dress, leaning over, gravity-defying, making a crazy arc in the air? Well, this was that, come to life, only backwards, in slow motion, and a hundred times sexier, with lots of leg, and with Nadia Comaneci instead. But a lot sexier. I already said that. I was having such wild fantasies during dinner. I kept knocking over wine glasses. Spilled three, broke two.

I mean, she is something, Cynthia. I'm frankly not sure I'm even up to the task. But I'm willing to try. Plus, you know, she's smart and funny and all the rest. In short, two words: Thank. You. Four more words: God. Bless. Cynthia. Amas. This coming from a devout agnostic, mind you. Maybe Tatiana Delaunay is my new religion. Wish me luck. I mean, *pray* for me. Ha. Goodbye."

Cynthia put away her phone and just savored everything for a moment. It was especially gratifying because Diego was one of her dearest friends.

Oh, man, I love my job. Now I just need to find the right woman for Jack Stone.

She caught up with him, who introduced her to Sternberg, who immediately, without even saying hello, asked if she had ever been in a movie and whether she'd be interested.

"Well, sure, I guess," she'd said.

"Okay, Jack," said Sternberg, "bring her by the studio next week. I think we have a role for her in that thriller." He turned back to Cynthia. "Have you done any acting before?"

"No, not really. Not since school."

"Good. I don't want an actress. This is a pretty big role, but it has to go to an unknown and you have the exact look I want."

"Listen, Steven," said Jack, "can I give Cynthia a little

tour? Is the bowling alley open?"

"Yeah, sure, go ahead," he replied. "Knock yourself out. I mean, don't really knock yourself out."

"Jack is always careful with his balls," said a guy with a cigar in his mouth.

"That's funny," said a cute young woman with a tiny bikini and gigantic martini, "I heard he was kind of reckless with them."

Cynthia and Jack headed through the kitchen door and across the lawn toward the large three-story colonial house known as the "game room."

"See what I have to put up with?" he asked. "It never stops."

"Poor baby," she said.

"Shut up," he replied.

"So what's this thriller he supposedly wants me in?" she said, skeptical, but flattered beyond belief. "Is that even real?"

"Oh, yeah, it's totally real," he said. "It's one of the films I'm producing with him. It's going into production in three months. That's the last major role to be cast I think. You get to kiss me in it."

"Lucky me," she said with the kind of gentle sarcasm that isn't sarcastic at all. In reality, she felt a little dizzy from the thrill of it all. She wasn't even looking for acting work. It was the furthest thing from her mind. It was amazing how things happen so easily, at such a whim, among certified grade-A gods of industry.

"Okay, back to the tour," he said, moving along. "This was the original home on the property when Steven bought it. He loved it and didn't want to tear it down. So——voila——the game room was born." He swung open the door and they entered what seemed to be a normal foyer of a normal single-family house. But when they walked through the entryway, they didn't come to a kitchen or a living room, they came to a basketball court.

"He has an outdoor court, but this is where they play when it's raining. Which, you know, around here is like five days a year, so it's good they have this because they play on it maybe *once* a year. Upstairs there's a dance studio and a badminton court. Third floor is for archery. There's a widow's walk on the roof that's really just for drinking and watching sunsets. They sometimes drink and fly kites from up there too. Drinking works with anything up there. The main thing is drinking."

"So, where's the bowling alley, Ol' Reckless Balls?"

"Oh, right. Just around here. It's my favorite part."

They walked across the basketball court and he opened another door, flipped a switch, and lights flickered on. And what lights. Neon and fluorescents delineated the interior space. This was a perfectly reconstructed 1950's style four-lane bowling alley, complete with swooping atomic-age car-culture lines, fins, all glistening metal and glass and naugahyde . . . a fantasy of Southern California futuristic architecture.

"Do you feel like doing a little bowling?" asked Jack, picking up a gorgeous swirled ball of aqua and ultramarine.

"Not really," she said. "I'd rather do a little talking." She really had to direct his attention to other women. To the perfect woman she knew she could find for him.

"Even better," he said. "Right this way." They walked across the room and exited once more into the sunlight, then down a winding stone path to another building. This one was more modern, like a small concrete bunker inset into the hillside. Its roof was covered by the most beautiful flower garden Cynthia had ever seen. They descended a small stairway and entered through an arched door.

"The screening room," he said.

It was dark and blue in there. Dim sconces lined the midnight-velvety walls and the theater seats were the same velvety blue. Everything in the room was elegant and understated, designed to disappear when the lights went out.

Jack led her to the back row, where they sat on a velvety blue chaise, obviously designed for maximum movie coziness for two.

"Wow," she said.

"Yeah," he said, "you're not kidding." He pressed a button on the armrest and a panel opened. He typed something in with a few quick keystrokes. The large screen glowed. "Steven believes that whatever else good movies are, they are only as great as their great moments. He has organized all his favorite films into moments, like best fight moments, best inspirational moments, best sex moments, etcetera. Watch this." He pushed a few more keys. "Best romantic moments. We can just watch it for a minute or two."

Talk about romantic moments. Cynthia was fully aware that she was being romanced. She wanted to restate her need to keep their relationship platonic and professional, but the elements of this day——the party, the people, being cast in a movie for god's sake——were conspiring against her.

He put his arm around her and they slipped down a bit, getting comfortable, preparing for an ocean of romance to roll over them. And roll it did. The very first scene that came up was from *The Apartment*, Cynthia's all-time favorite romantic moment: Shirley Maclaine running through the streets of Manhattan on New Year's Eve. Next: Chaplin, *City Lights*. Paulette Goddard, recently having had her eyesight restored by a benefactor whom she had never seen, now realizes it was the little tramp who sacrificed everything for her. *North by Northwest*, the stolen kiss in the wine cellar. *Say Anything*, the boom box scene. The moment when Zoey Deschenal kisses Joseph Gordon-Levitt at the copy machine in *500 Days of Summer*. Joseph Fiennes unwrapping Gwyneth Paltrow's forbidden femininity in *Shakespeare in Love*.

This was an amazing way to watch movies. Here, at this house, in this theater, sitting next to Jack Stone. *This* was one of those moments. She felt swept up in it, in spite of herself.

Jack shut the sound off, but kept the picture running. They turned toward each other. A lock of hair fell down across her face ala Veronica Lake. He reached over, tucked the strand behind her ear, and kissed her forehead. "Listen," he said, "I don't know what you want. I haven't even really known what I've wanted for a long, long time. That's why I contacted Second Acts. But I couldn't possibly find anyone I'd like more than you. I've never felt like this in my life."

"I know, Jack, I like you too, but . . ."

She *did* like him too. She had a burning curiosity about what it would be like to really know him, his body, his mind, and his heart. She had imagined being in that house of his, living that life, but more importantly, it felt like maybe she could really love him. She didn't know what she'd be feeling if Pete were still in the picture, but he wasn't. He was gone.

Jack's hand was on her cheek, his face so close, their noses gently touched. She didn't want to want him, but she did. He parted his lips, but spoke instead: "So, what did you want to talk about?"

"Just about you," she said. "We need to figure out exactly what you're looking for."

"There's nothing to figure out," he said. "I know exactly what I'm looking for." He kissed her. And it was good. The kind of kiss you think about later and remember forever.

As adamant as Cynthia was about keeping a professional distance, the physical distance between them had disappeared. Her head could not contact the rest of her. Bathed only in the flickering glow of silent celluloid romance, she felt herself slipping into an unavoidable denouement of a dizzying three-act structure. Act one had started the moment they'd met——their characters developing, their desire growing. Jack had known exactly what he wanted and——plot point one——he decided to get it. Throughout act two there were obstacles——his reputation, other suitors, a policeman, and a crazy mother on the phone——but they were summarily dismissed, overcome, vanquished, and left behind along the road, or high on a mountain top. Act three arrived with the party and, somewhere in there, Cynthia's dramatic and carnal needs had joined forces with Jack's.

They got up and Jack's clothes were suddenly off. He pulled her close. The rumors were *more* than true. He pressed his magnificent hard-on gently against her stomach, his heat seeming to melt the thin fabric of her summer dress away. He kissed her neck and shoulder, sliding his hand down, in and out of the small of her back, up and over her bottom to her thigh, pulling her dress up effortlessly, then delving down again under her panties and over her ass. He softly squeezed one cheek just right and held it there for a moment while sending his index finger on a scouting mission, delving gently, firmly into the delicate crevice between thigh and labia. He traced and retraced that lovely spot, never venturing over the lip, but instantly making her warm. And wet. And dizzy. She wondered if she would swoon. Her knees buckled slightly, but he held her firmly with his other arm and she felt confident that he would not let her fall. His fingertips circled around again, teasing the tender line between leg and lust. She felt something she'd never felt before. At first she thought it was his hand, but then realized the difference in their height and the length of his phallus made it possible. His harder-than-hard-on had poked through the opening between two of her dress's buttons and was nudging, caressing the underside of her left breast. As he slowly eased up onto his tiptoes, it reached her nipple, the meeting a hard and soft slippery kiss . . . lubricated by a generous pre-ejaculatory bead of semen. He was unbelievably adept at this. It was obviously not the first time he'd done it. She was so startled she wanted to back away to see it with her own eyes. But since both of his hands were accounted for——one still threatening to steal home, the other caressing her neck, then her cheek, then her trembling lips——she had all the confirmation she needed.

Cynthia felt his shaft against her belly, and imagined that length and that breadth inside her. It was something all right . . . like a separate being unto itself, his well-trained partner in this extraordinary assault upon her senses.

"Baby," he whispered, "I've never felt this way before."

This gave her pause.

He'd said almost the same thing moments earlier and she had sort of believed it the first time. Now, for Cynthia, something was off, not quite right. She didn't exactly doubt Jack's sincerity, but it all seemed too inevitable. Calling her *Baby* had rung untrue. Cynthia realized her hesitation wasn't even about him really. He was, without a doubt, a magnificent specimen. But during this final countdown, her thoughts had drifted to another place, far away, soaring 20,000 feet above the Pacific Ocean somewhere. Despite all the money and fame and fantastic surroundings, despite Jack being the one and only Jack Stone and all that came with that, Cynthia was thinking of Pete.

She pictured the freckly kid from high school, someone who wasn't even really her sweetheart--just a kid she really liked and with whom she shared a wonderfully embarrassing intimate afternoon twenty years ago. And she thought of the grown-up Pete, who she liked even more. Sweet Pete.

She reached down, intending to gently, politely push Jack away. But in the process, her palm grazed his famously massive missile and he instantly pressed himself more firmly against her, trapping her hand between this rock and hard place. This created the impression that she was grasping it. In fact, she *was* grasping it, less to further along his agenda and more to just hold it still, to contain it for a moment while she politely explained that she was sorry, but that Cynthia Amas, against all odds, was, that's right, was turning down the one and only Jack Stone for a second time.

But there it was. And despite the fact that she had decided not to continue, if truth be told, she was fine with holding onto it, if only for a moment. God, it was impressive. It seemed unreal. In the split second before she spoke, she automatically measured the circumference with her thumb and index finger. It was an unavoidable, instinctual calculation. And a strange sensation. Her thumb and fingertips did not meet. Did. Not. Meet. Again she was tempted to step away and take it in visually in all its glory, but she fought mightily against that impulse. This had to stop. It had already gone too far.

"Jack," she whispered, swaying a bit, holding him tightly but matter-of-factly too, trying desperately to sound clinically detached from the phallic phenom her fingers were currently clinging to like a mighty mast in a storm . . . this Moby Dick of dicks, this Titanic of Testosterone, this Rock of Fucking Gibraltar. She eased up on her grip, causing him to sigh ever so slightly, and making her realize that any movement at all would be interpreted as an intentionally erotic gesture. So she just froze where she was, her fingertips resting gingerly upon the head of his penis, the velvet hammerhead . . . business end of the gorgeously mammoth battering ram that would sadly, but necessarily, *not* be pounding mercilessly upon her castle gate, nor crossing her moat, nor coaxing her sweet surrender. But this too of course made him twitch with pleasure, inhaling quickly, then again and again . . . then releasing the word "Cynthia," like a man crying out for help, but in a whisper, like someone drowning in a library or church . . . desperate, but full of reverence, almost worship.

"Jack," she repeated, "I'm afraid I've made a terrible mistake. I can't do this. I can't make love to you. I can't do this to the man I love."

"But Cynthia," he murmured, sliding one hand up and over her hip, to her belly and breast.

"I know," she said, gliding her palm back down to the epicenter of his quaking, aching manhood, steadying him momentarily, as if attempting to calm a rocket mid-liftoff. "Listen. I realize this is beyond ridiculous and I'm sorry. But I can help you out. You know, with this."

She felt bad about it, but, then again, he would be getting the better end of the bargain. She was as turned on as he was . . . as ready to receive as he was to give. She was dripping for it. Aching for it. But she had decided it wasn't for her. Not here, not now, not with Jack Stone. She wanted it to be Pete. She wanted the cock in her hand, not to mention in her bush, to be Pete's.

She patted Jack's prodigious pulsating pistol from tip-top to stem to family jewels——a long, hard journey to be sure— —as if trying to tame a wildness that was far beyond taming. She was positive about ending things with Jack, but she had never been a cock tease. And at this stage it was becoming cock torture. She was a good person. She felt a sense of responsibility. And she was a big girl. She wasn't opposed to manually finishing a job she had clearly helped to start. Someone certainly had to do it. And it had all the telltale signs of a temporary term of employment. Not to mention that it would be kind of thrilling to witness. Like New Year's Eve in Times Square or a moonshot at Cape Canaveral. She and half the world would be more than willing to camp out for this sort of spectacle. Of course, there was also an element of Florence Nightingale to it . . . a selfless willingness to provide urgent care in a dire situation. Like administering first aid to a dying man. Which is what Jack picked up on.

"*Help me out!*" he shrieked, pulling away, his locked and loaded love cannon springing from her fingers and thwacking hard against his stomach. "You're kidding, right?"

"No, I'm sorry. That's the way it is. But really," she said, touching his chest tenderly with her open palm, "let me at least give you this nice parting gift."

He was hurt. But not so hurt to decline what she was offering. In his present state he would have accepted an invitation from anyone or anything.

And it didn't take long. Jack shuddered and collapsed onto the theater chaise in a rush of moans and cries and ungodly, quaking howls. It was extremely loud, incredibly close, and unbelievably messy. Cynthia thoughtfully sheltered the immaculate surroundings with the first thing she saw, a pink and black silk '50's-style bowling shirt with the word "Molly" embroidered on the chest.

Cynthia gazed upon him still writhing in pleasure, his arms

wrapped around his chest as if trying to ensure that his upper half wouldn't explode like his lower half had. She was pleased to have accommodated him. He really was positively Rodinesque to behold and, despite the fact that she was elated to have called whatever they'd started quits, she was also quite happy to have this moment with him. Not just because of the look of angelic bliss that graced his perfect features, nor the post-orgasmic aftershocks still rippling through him from head to toe. It also effectively freed her from the guilt she'd have inevitably felt if she'd simply left him hanging there. A hand job, even one of this size and caliber, is a very small price to pay for peace of mind. Of course, she'd left *herself* hanging there. She was on fire. She realized she was on the verge of ecstasy herself. She contemplated the possibility of excusing herself to "powder her nose" or "reapply lipstick," but ended up daydreaming for a moment about Pete instead, the warm ache down below merging with the larger one in her heart.

Day 2, Chapter 21

Molly Hannigan, Steven Sternberg's wife, passing by the theater door, heard what she thought was an animal in distress. She burst into the theater and turned on the lights.

"Hello! Who is it? Are you all right?"

"Molly!?" Jack cried, rolling off the chaise and running to her, his legendary phallus still partially erect, bobbing and weaving like a frightened garden snake.

It took Molly a second to focus on the nature of the scenario that was unfolding before her.

"Jack? What the hell? Jack? Why are . . . are . . . you . . ." she stuttered, then screamed, "Jack Stone is screwing some nobody in *my theater?!*"

"Hold on," he said, taking her hand, "let's not be hasty here."

"Wait a minute, Jack," said Cynthia, standing up and

crossing her arms across her breasts, "how are your first words not 'Cynthia is *not* a nobody!'?"

"Oh, come *on*, Cynthia! You know how I feel about you!" cried Jack, putting his arms around Molly, trying to comfort her, as she arched her back, trying to get away, squawking like an ostrich and pounding a drum solo on his chest. "But look at poor Molly here. This is no time to quibble about semantics."

Semantics? Poor Molly? Cynthia repeated in her head—— stunned, but somehow not surprised. This was Jack Stone. What did one expect? Sure, you can choose to dive into a convenient delusion with someone like him, or Max, but that's your choice. Ultimately she never really thought it could be any other way. And somehow, unlike Max, Jack still saw himself as innocent. He was so used to women throwing themselves at him, he had rationalized away his role and responsibility. Cynthia realized that *he* sincerely believed that all the women in his life were at fault. Of *course* he was fucking his best friend's wife. She had wanted it. She had asked for it. Like every other woman on the planet. Obviously.

It was also obvious to Sternberg, who was the next one through the door and whose nose was bleeding profusely, Jackson Pollock-ing all over his vintage Hawaiian shirt. Max was close behind, sporting a big black eye. More guests crowded in the doorway, rubbernecking for a view.

"Max?" said Cynthia, utterly dumbfounded. "What are you doing here? What happened to your eye?"

"A Steven Sternberg production," he said.

"Yes, well, as it turns out," said Steven, "I've been cuckolded by two——count 'em, *two*——of my guests. That I know of anyway."

"Wait," said Jack, releasing Molly from his arms, "Cynthia's brother was screwing you *too*?"

Max, no, everyone, looked at Jack like he was nuts. The impression was exacerbated when a line of semen dripped from the head of his half-mast monstrosity like a sad, slow-motion, milky teardrop. Everyone stared for a moment as the pearl-like weight of this viscous pendulum dangled at ankle level, dancing in response to Jack's every gesture.

"Can someone find this moron some pants?" asked Sternberg. "Or a home castration kit?"

Max turned to Cynthia. "Listen, darling. Sure, I had a little fling with Molly, here."

"A little fling?" shrieked Molly, "You call five years, two months, and eighteen days *a little fling*?"

That pretty much stopped all conversation, as everyone in the room considered the precision with which she described their history, while calculating what that history meant to them personally.

Cynthia smiled. "I feel like I should be taking notes for a tell-all something or other."

"Hold on," said Jack, turning to Max. "You're screwing Molly *and* your sister?"

But Jack was not even on Max's radar now. Neither was Molly, nor Steven Sternberg. Max was focused on Cynthia.

"Sin, please, listen to me, "he whimpered with hard-to-believe earnestness. "I'm the one who loves you. Jack Stone is a lying idiot."

"No I'm not!" said Jack. "I think I love her too. And at least I'm not screwing my sister!" The guy was genuinely confused.

Sternberg didn't know which of them to kill first. He glared at his wife, then Jack. "Stone, you can forget about those two movies in development. They're gone." Then he turned to Max. "I'm sorry. Who the hell are you?"

"I'm your wife's broker, Mr. Sternberg. Nice to finally meet you." Even now, under these dire circumstances, the irrepressible Max's lust for life was still intact.

It turned out that Steven Sternberg had only discovered that his wife even *had* a separate broker the night before. It had come to light that a little more than twenty-three million dollars had vanished. Poof.

So, regarding the question of whom to kill first, this was

the deciding factor.

He leaped at Max like a rabid chimpanzee, knocking him to the floor. Jack, still naked as a jaybird, joined the fray.

Molly was kicking at them all, ostensibly to break it up, but probably because she just really, really wanted to kick them. As for Cynthia, she watched with bemusement, happy she was getting out before she had fully gotten in. She loved watching Jack and his penis flailing around in the fray like that, though. It was a wonder. She thought of the nude male wrestling scene in the movie *Women in Love* and considered asking the other guys to strip as well, just for enhanced entertainment value. But it was already pretty damn good: the biggest movie star in the world fighting totally naked with the biggest director in the world. With special guest star, Max, her "idiot brother."

At least this chapter was over.

Day 2, Chapter 22

She realized she didn't care. She got dressed and walked around them all, squeezing through the crowd and into the bright California sunshine.

Cynthia found herself face to face with Lolita, who had been too far back to grasp what all the hub-hub was about.

"Lolita," said Cynthia, truly dumbfounded, "don't tell me you came with my crazy Max."

"Yeah, we bumped into each other in a bar, believe it or not," said Lolita. "I thought you wouldn't care, now that you're with Jack Stone. I mean, who would?"

"*With* Jack Stone," said Cynthia. "That's funny. I don't think anyone has ever *really* been with him. But, incredibly, despite all appearances, I think he actually wants it. And I swear I'll find him the right girl. It might just save his life." Her phone rang. "Hold on, I've gotta take this. Hello, Mom?"

"Cindy! You'll never guess where I am. Vegas, baby!"

"Mom. Tell me you did not just say 'Vegas, baby.'"

"Well, you'll never believe this. I'm engaged!"

"What? To who? Whom? What the hell are you talking about?"

"To Dominic, of course!"

"What? But, Mom! That's totally crazy! You can't marry Dominic! He's not marriage material!"

"Cindy, listen to me. We're celebrating our engagement by checking into the honeymoon suite. Oh, Dommy, look at all these mirrors! And rose petals!"

"What?" gasped Cynthia, nearly choking.

"What's that Dommy?" she asked her lustful husband-to-be, "'Put my roses on your piano, but put my tulips on your organ?' Tulips? Oh, *two lips! On your organ!* Ha! That's hilarious! Cindy, isn't that a scream?"

"Mom! That is definitely *not* a scream! That's Dominic! That's called *foreboding!* A bad omen! Wake up! You're supposed to take heed of shit like that!"

"Oh, relax Cindy. I'm just calling because we're going to hang around for a few days, test out this heart-shaped bed, and then come back to L.A. for a big engagement party at Marmont. And you're invited. But, honey, I've gotta go. Somebody has to drink all this champagne. And put her tulips on someone's organ. Bye!" *Click.*

Cynthia stared at the phone in disbelief. It almost seemed like the entire conversation had been some kind of joke . . . a crank call. But she knew it wasn't. She stuck the phone back into her purse, shook her head, and looked at Lolita. "My mom is supposedly engaged to be married."

"So I gathered," she said. "Which is weird, you know, because, I can't believe this, and it doesn't matter because I happen to know he's in love with *you*, but I think I'm falling for Max a little bit."

"You think you are falling for Max a little bit," deadpanned Cynthia. "A little bit." She giggled. It started slowly, as she tried to hold it in, but then it came in sharp blurts that transitioned into deep, rolling waves of laughter.

"Yeah, well, we had a lot of fun hanging out today," said Lolita, starting to laugh too. "I hope that doesn't bother you."

"Actually," said Cynthia, catching her breath and gesturing in the direction of the screening room. "It's much more likely to bother *you*."

Lolita instantly got it . . . that at least part of the fiasco going on inside the theater was Max-related. This made her laugh even harder.

Cynthia moved close to Lolita and they hugged long and hard, Lolita using one arm and clutching Wilfredo over to the side like a handbag with the other.

"Sorry that the madness of the past couple of days has put a strain on us," said Cynthia. "You know how much I love you and appreciate all your help with the business and everything else, right?"

"Yes and thanks and likewise," replied Lolita, kissing her friend gently on the cheek, then on the lips. "Celebrity makes everyone a little crazy, not just the celebrities."

Cynthia's phone rang again.

"Pete?" she answered, flabbergasted. "I assume you're calling from halfway around the world at this point?"

"Who's Pete?" asked Lolita. "Wait . . . *Pisco* Pete? Pisco and *Cheetos* Pete?"

But Cynthia didn't even hear her.

"No, actually," he said, "I got all the way to the airport and my flight was cancelled. I've been trying to call you. I left a message."

Just then, a beautiful, familiar young woman approached. "Cynthia, right?" she asked, moving in uncomfortably close. "You're the lady from Jack's house. His new *thing*."

Lolita looked at Cynthia. Everyone did.

"Pete," she said, "could you hold on for one second?"

Cynthia remembered the girl now. What in the world was she doing here? "Mariana, right? I didn't recognize you

without your clothes off. Listen, I was Jack's *almost* thing."
Then she pointed to the phone and said, "I'm this guy's thing
now. And he's mine."

"Oh, well that's good news," said Mariana. "Maybe I have
a chance with Jack after all."

"No," said Lolita, shaking her head. "You don't."

"Why?" asked Mariana. "And who *are* you anyway?"

"I'm the dog groomer," she replied.

"The dog groomer," sneered Mariana, wrinkling her nose
at Wilfredo. "Wait, so you're the idiot who fired Tanya?"

"No, well, yes, I am that idiot," said Lolita. "But I hired her
back. You know, kid, I don't know Jack Stone from jack shit,
but according to what Scarlett O'Hara told Wilfredo, you
might want to talk to Molly Hannigan before getting back
with him."

Mariana made a pretentious recent-Ivy-League-graduate–
talking-to-a-dog-groomer face. "What, pray tell, does my
stupid old *mother* have to do with anything?"

"Hold on again, Pete," said Cynthia, turning to Mariana.
"Your last name is *Sternberg*? You're Steven's *daughter*?"

"Yeah, so?"

"Wow," said Cynthia into the phone, "this is getting
positively *Chinatown*-ian."

Just as those words passed through Cynthia's lips, the

crowd parted and Molly Hannigan emerged from the theater. Her blouse was ripped and falling open, her face streaming mascara. There appeared to be a bite mark just above her left nipple, a crescent of dental indentations radiating redness, well on the way to black and blueness. She was trailed by Max, then Sternberg, then Jack——still stark naked, bright claw marks on his face and chest.

Then came cute martini-bikini girl. She was also in tears, another apparent Jack Stone casualty. Messily applied blood-like lipstick or actual blood adorned her perfectly pouty mouth.

Revelations kept unfolding for everyone, especially Mariana. It was hard to keep up, but she was a smart girl, getting smarter by the second: her Jack (not an unrequited infatuation, but actually her lover for the past six months), had been cheating on her with her best friend since grade school (Miss Martini-Bikini) and her mom, who had been *at least double*-cheating on her dad. Mariana assumed this was only scratching the surface, but at the moment she didn't feel the need to dig deeper. She rushed her mother, taking her down like a linebacker.

"So, it's true," said Lolita, her eyes focused like lasers on Jack's crotch-to-knee section. "And then some." Her mouth was wide open, as were the mouths of many other guests.

One elderly movie comedienne, about fifteen feet away, gasped, "Sweet mother of Jesus, that beats Milton Berle. And I should know. How I miss Uncle Miltie. That's what I called it." She reached out with one hand as if to touch it, cupping her breast with the other and swaying slightly. She seemed completely oblivious to the fact that everyone was completely aware of the nature of her pantomime and that she'd said all of that out loud.

Wilfredo leaped from Lolita's arms and took off like a teeny-tiny Rin Tin Tin.

"He's going to see Max," said Lolita. "He just adores that guy. Or, you know, he wants to steal his wallet."

But after leaping over Mariana and her mother——now working through their mommy-dearest nightmare by rolling around in the grass——Wilfredo ran right past Max. He ran past Steven Sternberg too. He leaped through the air, like some kind of canine superhero, and went straight for Jack Stone's you know what. Unlike almost everyone else, he apparently didn't like the look of him. Or it. Luckily, he was slightly off-target . . . down and to the right. He merely took a chunk out of his calf. Still, not a pretty sight.

This was followed by much running, screaming, yelling, bleeding, crying, 911-calling——a whole new level of mayhem. The stuff of Hollywood legend.

An ambulance was called. The party was over.

Cynthia was amazed. The three acts she'd outlined earlier were far from the real story, certainly not *her* story. Hers was still unfolding. The characters kept changing——dropping out, coming back, dropping out again. Bit players stole scenes from super stars. As much as she tried to wrest order from chaos, her narrative was weirdly stubborn. It refused to adhere strictly to the classical three-act structure. She couldn't even tell what act she was in half of the time.

"Pete?" said Cynthia, turning her back on the madness.

"Still here," he said.

"Um . . . I suppose you really have to leave."

"Yeah, our first gig is the day after tomorrow in Japan. A ten-hour flight and they're sixteen hours ahead. But my red-eye doesn't take off for another four hours. Do you want to come down here, maybe get a drink at LAX? It's *such* a romantic place to wait."

"Ah, *waiting*," she said, thinking back. "What was it? How long do I have to wait? Can I get you now or must I hesitate?"

"Exactly," said Pete. "And unless the airport bar is incredibly dark, we may have to wait until I get back."

"So be it," she said, "I'm calling a cab. Don't move."

She turned to Lolita and hugged her again. "See you soon . . . no doubt at the future Mrs. Dominic 'Lothario'

Orlando's engagement party. Did I just say that?" She rolled her eyes and turned, heading down the path.

Lolita and Wilfredo waved goodbye. Max approached and a very hyper Chihuahua wagged his tail like he was trying to achieve lift-off.

Max watched Cynthia walk out of his life, probably forever this time. "So, she doesn't like Stone. She likes this other guy."

"Seems like it," Lolita replied.

"And she *hates me*," he said. "Pretty much everyone does. Probably you too."

Lolita thought for a second, before saying, "Well, I'm sure there are *parts* of you I like."

"I can live with that," he said. "Speaking of parts, don't you think Stone's dick is just a bit *too* big? Sort of freakish? Women don't really like that, do they?"

"No, definitely not," she said, rolling her eyes. "Hey, handsome, how about you *take* me somewhere and *get* me a drink?"

"Can we ride your sweet pink Vespa?"

"How else are we going to get anywhere?" she asked, clutching Wilfredo to her breast, taking Max by the hand, and heading down the hill.

"Wait a minute," laughed Max, feeling around in his pockets. "I seem to have lost my wallet again."

"Damn it, Wilfredo" said Lolita, shaking her finger at the little dog and pulling the purloined item from her purse. "Here you go, Max."

"Umm . . ." he said, "all the cash is gone."

"It appears he ate it for lunch," smiled Lolita. "Poor baby hasn't eaten anything all day. Looks like we're taking *you* out."

"Even better," said Max. He was nothing if not good-natured.

They continued their way down the walk but were soon confronted by a large Irish Wolfhound and an enormous Great Dane.

"King and Max!" cried Lolita, on the verge of tears, "where did you come from?"

Max, the human, said, "Wait, the dog's name is Max?"

"Yes," said Lolita. "Max, meet Max. And King."

Max the human reached out his hand for both dogs to sniff.

"How did they even find you?" he asked.

"Who knows?" asked Lolita. "They're very special canines."

Both dogs growled menacingly.

"But, Jesus, Max, watch out. They're not to be trusted around men."

But Max kept his hand right there, three inches from the

dual jaws of death, holding it calmly, letting the beasts take their time.

The dogs hesitated for one more moment before licking Max's hand, forearm, elbow, and bicep . . . and then back to the hand to start again.

"Hmm . . . I think I passed the test," he said. "Now how are we going to transport them all on that scooter?"

"We'll take Wilfredo," said Lolita. "Somehow I think the other two will find their way." Then she thought of something. "Good god, Arthur!" She grabbed her phone.

Arthur picked up instantly. "Hello, Lolita, darling. I've been trying to call you. I screwed up. I lost the dogs. All three of them. King had me cornered in an alley and when I ran out of Kobe beef they all just took off. I left you tons of messages."

"No problem," said Lolita. "I found them. They're with me now. Thank you so much for all your help. You're the best. Hey, by the way, did I tell you about my friend's dating service? I think it might be perfect for you. I'll call you tomorrow. We'll have lunch and talk. Thanks again."

"Okay, sounds good," said Arthur, disappointed that Lolita still wasn't interested in him romantically, but knowing down deep that she never would be and truly appreciating her friendship and concern.

As the caterers and cleaning staff began the daunting task of restoring the Sternberg's trampled, bloody battlefield to its former pristine beauty, they heard a curious duet wafting its way up from the street, infused with the sweet smell of jasmine and orange blossom:

Nothing could be finer,

Than to be in your vaginer

In the mor-or-or-ning . . .

The lyrics made them laugh and they needed one. It quickly caught on, each of them eventually adding his own lewd verse. It made their work go faster. Who knows, it may have even led to some inter-staff romance later that night. Music and sex are both known as universal languages. Being bilingual would have to be even better.

Echoing through the canyon, over the sound of a puttering scooter, they swore they heard the three dogs singing along.

Day 2, Chapter 23

Cynthia's cab was cruising west on Sunset, heading for the 405. "Hesitation Blues" was on repeat in her head.

Buzz. The phone. Pete.

She picked up. "Hey."

"Where are you?"

"Just getting on the freeway."

"Because I had a couple of thoughts. First of all, what if you came along? For a week or something. I just checked . . . there are empty seats in first class and it's on me. A few days in Tokyo, a few more in Thailand . . . as long as you want. The first leg is basically island hopping throughout Asia."

She closed her eyes.

Oh, my god, a vacation sounds good. One with Pete sounds even better. Heaven, actually. What a great way to kick off a relationship.

She felt incredibly close to him already. It's like they'd known each other since puberty or something. Duh. And after today's festivities, she needed some Pete time. She was beyond horny. Maybe even beyond horngry.

Note to self: a girl can't spend that much time in the company of, let alone hanging onto, a near-equine-sized hard-on without getting just a little bit horngry. Jesus. A girl would need an assistant to wrangle that thing. A tractor trailer to haul it around. Maybe a second one for Jack's ego.

Despite everything, though, she was determined to find him a true love. But wow. She laughed out loud. Just thinking about Jack made her miss Pete even more.

"What is it?" he asked.

"Nothing," she whispered into the phone, "I was just thinking about how good island hopping with you sounds." But as she said it, she thought about the consequences and instantly talked herself out of it.

What are you thinking? You're moving into a new office in three days. You still have to hire an assistant. And supervise the last touches on the screening room. Buy furniture, video camera, editing software. Stock the kitchen. Deal with the website and scads of new clients. Fifteen interviews in the next six days. A million other small but crucial details. Plus you're starting a Second Acts blog. Sure, you've been brainstorming thoughts and concepts for weeks——*dating ideas, destinations, advice*——*but you have to go through with it and shape it . . . put it together in some sort of coherent fashion. You have nearly two thousand requests on Facebook that you haven't responded to yet. There's the personal page and the fan page. Maybe there should be a whole other one for industry people. Social networking is becoming a fulltime job unto itself. You really, really must find that assistant. Now. And then there's the little matter of a certain engagement party. Something you wouldn't mind missing, but wouldn't think of missing in a million years.*

"Pete, I'm sorry, but I can't. Not now. It's just impossible. But what was your other thought?"

"The other thought. Yeah. Well it turns out there's another flight leaving at 6:15 A.M. and I could catch that one instead and just make the concert. Meanwhile, there are plenty of hotels around here. There's gotta be one that's halfway decent. We could order room service. And then, you know, bleep all night."

Cynthia burst into laughter. It startled her a bit because it sounded exactly like her eighteen-year-old laugh.

"Book it, baby," she giggled. "God knows I'd like to bleep your brains out." She hoped the cab driver didn't gather what she was referring to, but he did. She could see him smiling in the mirror.

"I'm on it," said Pete in clipped military fashion. "Your final destination coordinates will be texted to you shortly."

"Very well," smiled Cynthia, slipping her phone into her purse and sliding deeper into the seat.

She gazed out the window and happened to see a young couple in a funky VW Beetle traveling alongside her. The adorable girl was driving and the adorable boy leaned over, first caressing the nape of her neck, then her arm, then nibbling at the flimsy strap of her translucent tank top. She smiled, staring straight ahead, wide-eyed, hands steady at 10:00 and 2:00, as he tugged the strap down over her shoulder with his teeth.

Cynthia was that girl.

She closed her eyes again.

She was behind the wheel, cruising quite a bit more than slightly over the speed limit toward her very specific predetermined destination while the hungry boy tugged and nibbled mercilessly at her defenses. He tasted her in places she didn't know she had places. He had an instinctual understanding of the geography of her longing . . . the topography of her desire. His eyes seemed custom designed to decipher the map of her heart. He pleaded for her to pull over, because he'd pinpointed *his* destination and it was *her*. They shared their champagne-soaked tongues as he wielded his hard wanderlust upon her between the soft sheets of a secluded hotel. His warm mouth melted away miles of wrong turns and dead-end streets. Back on the road, now he took his turn at the wheel and she was driven to distraction by the hungry hands of this romantic boy——a romantic boy with a big, proud, throbbing, loving hard-on with her name on it.

Maybe his name is Pete. And maybe against all odds their divergent highways were somehow merging. Maybe they had always been each others' destinations. Maybe not. Maybe she still wasn't quite ready to share the wheel with anyone at all. Too early to tell.

She recalled the wild parrot outside his window, the bright California landscape interrupted by this brighter flash of furious motion and sound. No matter what happened next there was something very special about the Cynthia-Pete equation . . . something familiar, like home, but with a mysterious spark, a thrilling flame caused by just the right kind of erotic and intellectual alchemy, just the right music floating on a warm breeze in a lush canyon at just the right time of day. Something like coming to an earthshattering mutual climax with a gorgeous time traveler in the bed you grew up in. Right there, on the very spot you dreamed those desires into existence for the very first time, when the world was new.

And here she was now. She opened her eyes.

"Driver," said Cynthia, sitting up a bit, "doesn't this thing go any faster?"

The End